Sacrifice

KATEE ROBERT

Published by Sourcebooks Casablanca, an imprint of Sourcebooks
P.O. Box 4410, Naperville, Illinois 60567-4410
(630) 961-3900
sourcebooks.com

Also published as part of *Court of the Vampire Queens* in 2022 in the United
States of America by Sourcebooks Casablanca, an imprint of Sourcebooks.

Cataloging-in-Publication Data is on file with the Library of Congress.

Printed and bound in the United States of America.
POD

To everyone who was Team Damon, Team Spike, and far too into Dimitri Belikov.

Sacrifice is a dark and incredibly spicy book that contains dubious consent, blood play, patricide, pregnancy, blood, gore, murder, explicit sex, vomiting (caused by pregnancy), discussions about abortion, abusive parent (father, historical, off-page), attempted sexual assault (alluded to, nongraphic), and attempted drugging.

1

I DON'T WANT TO BE HERE.

Rain slashes my face, the wind turning my long hair into whips. I feel like I've been walking for hours, but I suspect in the light of day, I'll discover it's a mere half mile from the tall iron gate to the front steps of the house looming in front of me. It looks like something out of a gothic novel, towering peaks and narrow windows, all dark and vaguely faded as if it's stood on this hill for time unknowing.

Probably because it has.

I readjust my grip on my suitcase and march up the steps. There's no point in turning and running as far and fast as I can. I already tried that and it got me a brand-new scar on my knee and a limp that made the hike up here agonizing. The only reason my father healed me the little bit that he did was to keep me from being fully damaged goods. The man in this house won't care about a few scars. He's interested in what lurks beneath my skin.

Specifically, my blood.

I don't knock. The vampire in this house knows I'm coming. There's no point in playing the courteous guest or pretending I want this. I make it three steps inside before the door slams shut behind me, sealing off the roar of the storm and leaving only eerie silence in its wake. I glance over my shoulder, but I don't expect to see anything.

Vampires move faster than the human eye can see. And while I'm only 50 percent human, I'm tainted by that lineage enough to not be able to see more than a blur of movement. Another way I'm seen as damaged goods. At least if I had full vampire reflexes and strength, it might make up for my lack of magic. As it is, I'm barely better than a human. Barely better than prey.

The knowledge sticks in my throat, preventing a shriek of surprise when I turn around and find a man looming close. No, not a man. A *vampire*. It's there in his pale skin, the barest hint of fang pressing against his bottom lip. It's the slightest loss of control, and it makes me wonder how long it's been since the last sacrificial lamb was sent to this house.

He's gorgeous in the way all vampires are, flawless beauty and hidden strength. This one has dark brown hair that falls in a sleek wave to his shoulders, fathomless dark eyes, and a muscular body slightly too thin for his frame. He holds himself stiller than any human ever could. "I apologize."

I blink. Of all the things I expected him to say, that didn't number among them. "What?"

"Cornelius sent you."

It's not a question, and I can't quite stifle the flinch at my father's name. At the reminder of who I can blame for my current circumstances. "Yes."

"You know why."

Now his stillness makes sense. He's barely preventing himself from attacking me. My heartbeat kicks up, and I can see well enough in the dark to note how his nose flares as he inhales my scent. I'm running out of time. I want to stay silent, but there's no point. Despite my best efforts, my voice wobbles a little with nerves. "He gave me to you."

"Yes." It's hardly more than a sigh. "We'll discuss this... after."

"After—" This time I can't stop the shriek of surprise. One blink he's a few feet away, and the next he hits me with the force of a runaway truck. He still manages to control our fall so I don't bash my head on the marble floor, but I don't have a chance to appreciate the consideration. Not when he surges forward and bites my neck.

"Fuck!" My curse turns into a breathy moan. I knew to expect this, but being lectured on the pleasure of a bloodline vampire's bite does nothing to translate how *good* it feels. It's as if every pull of his mouth is connected directly to my clit, pulsing through my body and turning my resistance liquid. I don't *want* to want this, but my body doesn't care. I arch against him, reaching up to pull him closer to me.

One of his hands is in my hair, using the leverage to keep my neck bared to him, and the other snakes around to press against the small of my back, urging me closer to him. As if I wasn't already straining against him.

I have the distant horrified thought that I'm going to come if he doesn't stop. "Wait!"

"I'm sorry." I feel more than hear his murmur. His tongue strokes my neck and then he moves to the other side. "I can't stop."

"But—"

He bites me again and I whimper. Fuck, that feels good. My dress is tangled up around my hips and I wrap my legs around his waist, arching closer. I can feel my blood warming his cool body, and evidence of his bite is already hardening against me. He rolls his hips and growls against my skin, but he doesn't move his hands from their spots. He doesn't touch me like I'm suddenly desperate for him to do.

"More," I moan.

He gives a hard pull to my neck and I slide my hands down his back to his ass, holding him close as I roll my hips, grinding myself on his hard cock like a wanton thing. It doesn't matter I'll regret this later, I'll hate both him and me for this loss of control. I need to come more than I need my pride. It will still be there on the other side of this.

I work myself against him, and I have half a thought to reach for the front of his pants, but it would mean stopping this delicious friction, and I'm not willing to do that. Another time.

It's what I'm here for, whether I chose this role or not.

I realize he's stopped sucking my blood, but the endorphins have nowhere near worn off. I should stop. I know I should stop, but the subtle pressure of his fingertips against the small of my back urge me on. Pleasure winds through me, tighter and tighter, and for one breathless moment, I think I won't get there, that I'll be poised on the brink for an eternity.

My orgasm hits me even harder than the vampire did earlier and I come more intensely than I ever have before, crying and panting as I hump him like I really do want this. The last wave crests and I slump back to the cold marble floor, my head feeling fuzzy and too light. "You took too much," I murmur, my words coming as slowly as taffy.

His tongue strokes my neck and he gives another of those growls I don't want to enjoy. "You don't taste like a human."

It's strange to be having this conversation on the floor while he's pressing between my thighs, but I can't seem to find the energy to shove him off. "I'm not." I lick my suddenly dry lips. "I'm half bloodsucker."

"Ah." He inhales and slowly, oh so slowly, he releases me and sits up. There's a new flush in his pale cheeks and his eyes are blazing with power. He kneels between my legs and his gaze strokes over me in a way I can almost feel, lingering on my lips, on my bloody neck, where my breasts are nearly escaping this ridiculous dress, where said ridiculous dress isn't covering my panties any longer. My panties that are *soaked*.

I start to cover myself, but he catches my wrists, easily over-powering me. He does another of those long inhales and I know beyond a shadow of a doubt he's scenting my arousal. He shifts my wrists to one hand and reaches for my panties with the other.

"Wait!"

The vampire's eyes are pure black and his fangs are on full display. The little glimpse of control from earlier, of regret, are nowhere in evidence. Gods, I'm in trouble. His gaze drops to my panties again. "You know why you're here." His knuckles brush the wet fabric, lightly stroking against my pussy. Despite just coming, I have to fight the desire to lift my hips in invitation. I *know* it's the aftermath of the bite, but I hate myself a little for it.

He pauses, his hands shaking as if he's fighting himself. He could have broken my wrists, could do so much more damage, and there's nothing I could do to stop him. "Say it."

I don't want to. I very much don't want to. But the words spill from my lips, almost as if he compelled them with his low voice. "I'm here to satisfy your hunger."

"Hunger*s*, little dhampir. All of them." He strokes me again. "Lift your hips."

I obey even as I argue. "You said we'd talk."

"Yes, after." Still, he hesitates. A drop of blood drips down his chin and I dazedly realize he's bitten himself. "Say yes."

The fact that he isn't simply taking what he obviously wants confuses me even as I hate him for making me say it. Would he really stop if I tell him to? I'll never know. "Yes."

His eyes flash to my face as he grips the crotch of my panties and tugs them down my legs. He could have just ripped them off—it probably would have taken less effort—and that little show of restraint almost makes this worse. Or better. I'm honestly not sure.

I didn't choose to be in this house, to be a sacrificial lamb, but that doesn't stop my body from shaking with need. I bite my bottom lip as he moves down my body and I know I should argue more, should never have let the word *yes* leave my lips, but he gives my pussy another of those light strokes and the touch short-circuits my brain.

"Please," I whisper. I don't know what I'm begging for, for him to stop or not stop. It doesn't matter. He shifts slightly to the side and strikes, quick as a snake, sinking his fangs into the sensitive skin of my upper thigh.

I come again instantly.

I keep coming, wave after wave, until I'm sobbing and begging, but I can't begin to guess what I'm begging for. For him to stop. For him to fuck me. It doesn't matter. Before I can decide, he lifts his head.

And then he's gone, a flash of motion up the curving staircase, and I'm left alone in the entrance hall. Wet. Bleeding. And filled with enough confusion that my head feels like it's spinning wildly on my shoulders. "What the *fuck* just happened?"

2

I THINK I BLACK OUT. I MUST, BECAUSE ONE MOMENT I'm lying on the cold marble floor and the next I'm blinking up into a darkened bedroom. I go perfectly still out of habit, forcing my heartbeat to slow and my breathing to stay even. I can see well in the dark, courtesy of my vampire blood, and I pick out the features of a bedroom that must have been the height of luxury sometime in the last few hundred years. It hasn't been kept up in the meantime. There's dust on every surface of the heavy wooden furniture and the canopy overhead is filled with holes and worn nearly transparent.

I count to one hundred slowly and then do it again.

Nothing moves in the room except for the steady rise and fall of my chest.

I can't lie here forever, no matter how much part of me wants to curl into a ball and wait for this all to be over. Maybe another woman in my position would. Maybe the last sacrifice sent to this place did.

It's not who I am.

My life has been hell since I was old enough to realize my position within the vampire colony my father rules. I am the worst of all things. Magic-less. Bastard. The product of my monster of a father and one of his human mistresses he pretends is there of her own free will, rather than an exotic pet he likes to keep to prove his power. Unlike other dhampir children of bloodline vampires, I have no magic to speak of. I fit nowhere, so every move I made was an insult deserving punishment.

For years, I didn't understand why he resisted killing me and getting me out from underfoot once and for all.

Now, I do.

This is where he planned to send me all along. A sacrificial lamb. A womb just waiting to be filled with one of the failing vampire bloodlines my father holds so highly. And if I die before accomplishing that? He'll lose no sleep over it.

Under other circumstances—mainly, if I'd inherited his magic like I should have—my getting pregnant would make me his heir. Now, he wants me to serve as a vehicle to bring another bloodline under his control. It seems particularly cruel, but I've long since stopped expecting anything resembling kindness from my father.

I let rage propel me to sit up and gingerly touch my neck. The bites are small puncture wounds. The vampire didn't so much as tear my skin, though I'm not about to thank him for it.

Him.

Malachi Zion.

If my father is to be believed, this vampire can trace his bloodline back to one of the original seven vampires. There are only two types of vampire: turned and bloodline. Over time, the number of turned vampires has far outnumbered the bloodline ones born—something rare even before vampires withdrew and hid away from humans, and now practically nonexistent—which means those family lines are in danger of dying out.

Which is supposedly where I come in.

I sigh and climb carefully off the bed. My thigh aches, but my busted knee aches worse. The hike did me no favors. I limp to where my suitcase is tucked near the door. It appears untouched, but when I lay it down and open it, I find things rifled through. "Nosy ass vampire," I mutter. A quick search finds what I feared. He's taken my knife. I glare at the mess of clothing in the suitcase. "What's the fucking point? You're like two hundred years old, and I'm half human. I couldn't kill you with that knife if I tried."

If he's lurking close enough to listen to me rant, he makes no appearance to reveal it. It's just as well. Even with my vampire side accelerating my healing, I'm a little light-headed from blood loss. I need to eat something, but I might as well wish on a star as hope that kitchen is stocked.

Still.

The alternative is hiding in my room until the vampire starts wanting a snack and seeks me out again. My body hums at the thought, entirely too on board with the idea. I'd heard bloodline vampires had a pleasurable bite, had even seen it play out during my father's *services* when he moves through the room and bites a few of his chosen followers, but I chalked it up to vampire-on-vampire nonsense. The few times I haven't been fast enough to avoid one of the turned ones' fangs, it *hurt*.

I glance at the bed, at the reminder I'm here as more than blood donor. All part of my father's grand plan to bring the vampire race back to supremacy or some bullshit. He never asked me what *I* want, but then a bastard magic-less dhampir is more tool to be utilized than actual person from where he's standing. I clench my fists.

The house will be watched. My father is too smart to leave anything to chance. He figures if he throws me in this place, it's only a matter of time before Malachi either knocks me up or kills me. Either will suit his purposes. If I *do* get pregnant, I suspect I won't live past the live birth. It won't matter if my child manages to inherit powers or if they are born without magic like their mother. I'll have served my role.

Fuck that.

I'll find a way out of here, even if I have to carve my way through Malachi and every vampire guarding this house. I need to bide my time and wait for the right opportunity. I doubt I can kill them, but I should be able to find a way to incapacitate them long enough to get the hell out of Dodge.

First things first. I won't be worth a damn while I'm dizzy and exhausted.

I glance at the bed again and shake my head. Even without the sheer amount of dust and moth-eaten fabric, there's no reason to make it easier on the vampire. *No reason to tempt myself, either*. I won't be sleeping there.

I dig a power bar out of my suitcase. I only stashed a handful, which means I *do* need to figure out food at some point.

Starving to death is not on my agenda. A faint sliver of light trickles through the window. I push wearily to my feet and move to look outside. Dawn is here. And I'm on the second floor. I try to open the window, but it's been painted shut. Great. Not that I expected much else. If this house has been updated since it was built, I haven't seen any evidence of it.

Now I'm stalling.

I grit my teeth and open the bedroom door. Nothing happens. Just like nothing happens when I step out into the hallway. It looks just like the entranceway and the bedroom—old and dusty and threadbare. The carpet beneath my shoes is black or purple or maybe gray. It's hard to determine in the low light and with age fading it. The walls are equally faded, though I can tell they were originally green. Paintings line them, but I ignore the art for now. Getting caught up in curiosity isn't an option.

I find the front stairs easily enough. This place seems laid out logically, which is a relief in a way. Not that I know what I'm supposed to *do* with that information. For all my dreams of running, there are several harsh realities standing in my way.

First and most insurmountable is the vampires themselves. They're faster than me. Stronger than me. And all of them, from Malachi to my father to the guards no doubt lingering at the edges of the property, have a vested interest in me staying trapped exactly where I am.

But it's more than that. The only things I know about human society are what I've gleaned from the few servants my father keeps and the books my mother somehow managed to smuggle into the colony. It might be enough to whet my appetite for freedom, but I'm not naive enough to think I'm anywhere near prepared to slip into their world.

Knowing all that won't stop me looking for an escape, but it's enough to keep me from doing something truly reckless. Like trying to flee right now, this morning.

The kitchen is slightly more updated than the rest of the house. The appliances look like things I recognize, and there's power when I flip on the lights. I study the dusty hanging lights. "So the bloodsucker likes a little modern convenience after all." Apparently he has some way to order in resources, which is useful knowledge to have.

"Such charm you have, little dhampir."

I startle like a cat, straight up into the air and over a good six feet. The vampire doesn't move from where he's standing against the doorframe I just walked through. He looks...amused. And healthier. There's a flush to his pale skin from *my* blood.

The thought sends a pulse through my body, directly to my core. I didn't hate being his snack as much as I want to, and even as I tell myself I'll fight him to a standstill before I let him bite me again, part of me wants it and wants it now.

Part of me wants *more*.

I glare, hating that now *my* face is flushed. "If you drink any more from me, you'll kill me and my father will probably make you wait another twenty-five years before he sends a replacement."

The vampire—Malachi—pushes off the doorframe and takes a purposefully slow step into the kitchen. He looks like he's concentrating, as if it's more natural for him to move too fast for me to really see. "You're here for a reason. Don't forget that."

"Why not tattoo *sacrifice* on my forehead in case I forget?"

His brows inch up. "The last one wasn't so mouthy."

"And look what happened to her." I don't know much about the stranger who occupied this position before me. Only that she was chosen to continue Malachi's bloodline and my father was infuriated by her inability to breed—and stay alive. I'm not even sure how long ago it was. "Thanks, but if I'm going to die in this house, I refuse to cower for the time I have remaining."

His sensual lips curve, and I loathe I notice they're sensual at all. "Are you mad I didn't fuck you earlier?"

My jaw drops. "You're out of your fucking mind!" I throw my hands up when he drifts another step closer. "I didn't even want you to bite me."

"Mmm." Another step. I retreat and he stalks me through the kitchen. He's edging me back into the corner of the counter, and there's not a damn thing I can do about it. He finally stops a bare six inches from me and braces his hands on the counter on either side of my body. This close, it's impossible not to notice, no matter how run-down the house, *his* clothing is new and smells faintly of tobacco and something spicy. He wears a pair of fitted pants and a shirt that would be at home on some historical romance about a pirate. It leaves a slice of his pale chest bare, and I can see a number of raised scars there.

It looks like someone tried to hack out his heart.

"I've tasted a lot of humans over the years." He sounds almost like he's musing to himself. "Even a few dhampirs before you." His gaze coasts down my body, lingering on my breasts. "None of them tasted as good as you."

I blink. "Is that supposed to be a compliment?"

"It's a fact." He shifts another inch closer. "It intrigues me."

"Back off." My voice comes out hoarse. My skin is tingling and I wish I could say it's tingling with danger or fear. It'd be a lie. I'm fighting not to press my thighs together from the remembered pleasure.

Malachi leans down a little until he's looking directly into my eyes. His eyes are so dark, they seem to draw in the light of the room. There's a hunger lurking there, and I can't stop the horrified suspicion he's seeing that hunger reflected right back at him when he looks into my eyes.

His lips curve slowly. "You don't want me to back off."

"Wait."

"You keep saying wait, little dhampir. Not stop. Shall I slow down further?" He lifts his right hand with agonizing slowness. I stand perfectly still as he traces his thumb over my collarbone to the thin strap of my dress. Now's the time to say stop. I don't know if he'll respect it, but I should voice it all the same. Should tell him how much I loathe his touch. How much I never want him to lay hands on me again.

I don't.

I hold my breath and lift my chin.

He eases the strap off my shoulder and down, tugging it until the fabric falls to bare my breast. The cool air of the kitchen pebbles my nipple. Or that's what I tell myself as he stares down at me. Using that same exaggerated slowness, he moves to my other shoulder and gives it the same treatment until I'm naked from the waist up.

Malachi's gaze flicks to my face, and whatever he sees there has him licking his lips. "You know why you're here."

He said the same thing to me multiple times last night. As if he's checking in with me, which is laughable. He's no different from my father, from all the other vampires I've been forced to interact with over the twenty-five years of my life. He wants what he wants, and he'll mow down anyone who gets in his way. Including me. *Especially* me.

My anger blooms again, ready and waiting for the least provocation. I glare. "Just call me your resident blood bank and womb. Suck me, fuck me, do whatever you want. It's not like I'm a real person to you. I'm just a *little dhampir*, after all."

"You're *my* little dhampir now." He brackets my waist with his hands, his fingers digging in the slightest bit.

I have the borderline hysterical thought he could literally rip me limb from limb right now and there's not a damn thing I could do about it. Wouldn't *that* ruin my father's day? I laugh. I can't help it. It comes out angry and derisive. "I might have been traded like a possession, but I'm not yours. I never will be."

"I suppose we'll see, won't we?" He closes the last bit of distance between us and I lose my grip on my rage. It shudders out of me in a sigh that's almost a whimper. Malachi's so *strong*. I don't know why that surprises me. All vampires are stronger than they look. Hell, so am I, even if I can't compare to a full-blood. But there's something about the way he touches me, as if tempering that strength so he doesn't harm me sends my body into a dizzying spiral into desire.

I am so fucked.

3

"I'M FEELING GENEROUS."

I stare up at Malachi's handsome face. "What?" I should be fighting right about now, but the only thing I'm fighting is my desire to arch against his hard body.

He flashes a little fang in a quick grin. "I'll let you choose where I bite you this time, little dhampir. But only if you speak quickly."

"You can't." I sound like I'm asking a question rather than giving a command. I lick my lips, achingly aware of the way he follows the movement. "Unless you really do want to kill me."

"I'm not hungry for your blood." He leans down and his lips brush against the shell of my ear. "I want to feel you come again."

I open my mouth, but not a sound emerges. I expected a lot

of things when my father laid out my fate in that cold way of his. Pain. Torment. Maybe even death. I didn't expect this. I'm not even sure what *this* is. "What?"

"I can bite you here." He gives my neck a slow kiss, dragging his mouth over the spot where he bit me last night. Malachi keeps moving down, stopping at the top of my chest. "Or here." His gaze flicks to my face and he descends to flick his tongue out and stroke my nipple. "Or here."

"Do it." I don't even sound like myself. I sure as hell don't feel like myself. It takes everything I have not to reach for him as he holds my gaze and sinks his fangs into the soft skin of my left breast just above my nipple.

Pleasure bows my back and I cry out. Gods, it shouldn't be *so good*. And then his mouth closes around my nipple and it gets even better. He cups my other breast and loops his free arm around my waist, pulling me tighter against him. He strokes me with his tongue and I'm lost.

I barely register letting go of the counter. One second I'm clinging to it for dear life and the next my fingers are tangled in his long dark hair, holding him to me. My knees buckle, and he eases us to the floor with me straddling him. Careful. He's so fucking *careful*. He's not really taking blood right now, not more than a few drops. His hold on me is tight, but nowhere near tight enough to hurt me.

Like before, each pull of his mouth sends a bolt of lust directly to my clit. I whimper and arch closer. "Please." I'm so empty. I need to come. I need to fuck, hard and quick. I simply need.

He shifts his grip around my waist, urging me down until

I'm pressed against his cock. He's hard again, and I have the dazed thought that he's massive, but I can barely cling to it. Not when he rocks me against him, sliding my pussy along his length through his pants. It's not enough, but it feels too good to stop.

Over and over again, building my pleasure stroke by stroke, pull by pull of his mouth.

He releases my breast and I cry out in protest, but Malachi moves to my right one. This bite is a little rougher, and it propels me into a brutal orgasm. I cry out and grind down on him, coming so hard he has to tighten his hold to keep me from collapsing. He licks my nipple one last time and lifts his head.

I look down and find twin bite marks marring my breasts. Thin trickles of blood run from each puncture wound, and the sight threatens to ramp up my desire again. Especially when he leans down and drags his tongue over my skin, cleaning me.

Now's the time to say something. To remind him again I'm not here because I chose to be. I don't actually want this, humping him in the kitchen notwithstanding.

Malachi looks up at me and gives that slow smile. "Don't worry, little dhampir. I *will* fuck you, and soon. This was simply a little taste of what it will be like."

There's no point in protesting. He *will* fuck me. It was inevitable from the moment I walked through the door, but it feels almost like fate in this moment. A fate I'm not quite sure I want to fight. If it's this good with a bite and most of our clothes on, will it be better when we're both naked and I'm entirely at his disposal.

Will I survive it?

Vampires can go into a frenzy when they fuck. It doesn't happen often as long as everyone's getting regular feedings, but Malachi has been alone in this house for at least as long as I've been alive. I don't know why he doesn't hunt, but the last sacrifice my father sent was before I was born. No matter how good his control right now, it might not hold.

He might kill me.

"Let me go," I say quietly.

He slowly releases me and leans back to prop his hands on the floor. He's studying me like I'm a puppy who's done something unexpected. "You enjoyed what just happened."

Yes, I did. A lot. I also want it to happen again as soon as possible. I have too much self-preservation to admit as much, though. "Your bite is orgasmic. Of course my body liked it."

"Ah."

I need to get up, especially when I can feel his cock pulsing against me, but my legs aren't cooperating. Or that's what I tell myself as I glare at him. "And stop ambushing me. I get you need blood, and that's what I'm here for, but unless you want this sacrifice to be short-lived—literally—you need to knock that shit off."

His brows inch up, and he's back to looking like he's half a second away from laughing at me. "I'll take that into consideration."

"I'll need food, too." I brace my hands on his shoulder to push to my feet, but somehow my wires get crossed and I rock my hips against him. Just a little. I bite my bottom lip. "What are you *doing* to me?"

"Nothing." He very slowly, very gently, replaces his hands on my hips. "Nothing at all."

"I don't believe you." My desire is spiking again, my body hot and pliable. I have to get out of here, and I have to do it now. Otherwise I'm in danger of doing something unforgivable, like reaching between us to free his cock and taking him deep inside me. I want it. I want it more than I want my next breath.

I shove to my feet.

Or at least I try.

My bad knee buckles halfway up, and Malachi catches me before I make harsh contact with the floor, his hands beneath my knees. I barely have a chance to register what happened when he moves us, lifting me up and setting me on the counter. He pushes my dress to bare my knee and frowns at it. "This is recent."

No point in denying it. The truth is written right there on my skin in ugly purple scars. "Yes."

"I was under the impression dhampirs heal quickly."

"Not as quickly as vampires."

"That is not an answer."

He's like a dog with a bone. I don't understand where he's headed with this line of questioning. "Yes, I heal quickly."

"And yet you have an injury like this." His face takes on a forbidding look. "Explain."

Oh, for fuck's sake. I shove at his shoulders, but I might as well try to shove a mountain. Frustration bubbles up inside me, hot and cloying. "As I'm sure you've probably figured out, I didn't exactly volunteer for this gig. I tried to run. My father made sure I wouldn't be able to again."

He goes still in that predatory way that makes every instinct I have scream at me to flee, which might be laughable under other circumstances. Flee. Sure. That'll work out great.

Malachi's thumb traces the most prominent bit of the scar, the spot where my father beat my knee again and again until the bones were little more than pebbles. "There is no quick fix for this type of injury."

"Thanks for that, Doctor Malachi, but I'm already aware. Even with my accelerated healing, I'll never walk right again." It's something I can't think too closely about or it might be the thing that breaks me. My entire life has been spent running, even if it was contained within the colony walls. I've escaped beatings and worse because of my ability to flee. No longer.

He presses a hand to the center of my chest. "Stay."

"I am not your dog to command."

"Stay," he repeats.

I don't know why he bothers to tell me what to do. He moves so quickly, I barely have a chance to tense before he's back between my thighs again, this time holding a knife. I freeze. "A vampire with a knife. How novel." Which reminds me. I narrow my eyes, trying to ignore the blade glinting between us. "Return *my* knife."

"When I'm sure you won't try to carve out my heart, I will."

"Looks like someone already tried and botched the job." I jerk my chin at the mangled scars on his chest. "I'm more than happy to do it properly."

He chuckles, a dry rasping sound. "What's your name, little dhampir?"

As much as I want to dig in my heels instead of answering, it won't serve any purpose. I'm here for the foreseeable future. Might as well be on a first-name basis with my captor, willing or no. "Mina."

"Mina." He says it slowly. "It suits you."

"If you say so."

Malachi reverses the knife in a smooth move and presses it to the side of his throat. "You seem like a smart girl."

I blink. "Um."

"Too smart to deny yourself a tool, even if I'm the one giving it to you."

I don't know he's right about that, but I can't help staring at his throat as he drags the tip of the knife over his skin, leaving a thin trail of blood in its wake. My fangs ache in response. I might not require blood the way actual vampires do, but the desire is still there. "What are you doing?"

"Blood is power, little dhampir." He leans in, pressing against me, until his neck is a few spare inches from my mouth. "Drink from me enough and your knee will mend itself."

"Impossible." I throw the word out like a life preserver. "It's healed already."

"Not impossible." He tilts his head to the side, baring his neck completely. "Drink."

I shouldn't. It's another tie linking me to him. His bloodline's power might not be glamour like my father's, but sharing blood back is what vampires do to mind-fuck humans. I've never drank from a vampire before. I don't know what will happen if I do.

But if he's not lying... If it *can* heal my knee...

My tongue snakes out without permission and drags over his neck. That small taste feels like a nuclear bomb going off inside me. I stop thinking, stop trying to rationalize my way through this. I simply act.

I bite him.

I have no finesse, like he demonstrated even when he was tackling me to the floor that first time. I'm too desperate for more.

His blood is like lightning on my tongue. It lights every nerve ending up. I swear I can actually feel the power rolling through my body. I want more.

Malachi digs his hand into my hair and gently pries me off him. "That's enough."

"But—" I can't take my eyes off his neck. Even as I watch, the wounds close. "More."

"Not today." He steps back slowly, as if it pains him to put distance between us. "Get some sleep, Mina. You're going to need it."

I inhale. Even the air tastes different with his power flowing through my veins. "I don't want to sleep. I want to..." I look at him. He really is sexy in a brutal sort of way. I can appreciate that, appreciate his strength and the way his eyes bleed to black when he looks at me. "I want to fuck."

"Not that, either."

"Why not?" Is this what being drunk feels like? It's completely different from the bliss of his bite. That's a physical thing and it eases almost as soon as his fangs leave my skin. This feeling is in my veins, searing me right to my very soul. I shiver. "It's what I'm here for, isn't it?"

"Yes." He's studying me, but I'm too loopy to read his expression. "But not yet. If you still want my cock when you wake up, you're more than welcome to it."

"I want it now." I hop off the counter, but the world shifts, turning topsy-turvy on me. My bones go liquid and the last thing I feel before darkness claims me is Malachi's strong arms closing around me.

4

I WAKE UP IN THE SAME BED AS BEFORE. UNLIKE LAST time, I don't feel like I've been hit by a truck. I feel *great*. Like I've had a full night's sleep and a month's worth of well-balanced meals. I sit up slowly and look down. My dress is back in place, but a quick check shows the bite marks are healed as if they never existed.

I prod my knee, but though the pain is fainter than normal, I don't feel much different. Maybe it was all bullshit, but I can't deny I feel better than I have in months.

Maybe that's the point, though.

Biting him drugs me as much as his bite does. The first dose was free, but he'll demand I fuck him for another.

The thought should fill me with horror. Having sex with Malachi means playing out the scheme my father put into motion. But the thought feels distant. Malachi isn't anything like

I expected. Oh, he's vampire through and through—arrogant and predatory and sure that might makes right. But if he was as much monster as my father is, he would have taken *everything* he wanted from me that first time in the foyer. He'd have chained me to a bed somewhere and gotten down to business until I'm knocked up or dead.

But just because Malachi is taking a softer route doesn't mean he's a better person. I have to remember that. Even if part of me feels a thrill of anticipation at the thought of his hands on me again.

I climb carefully to my feet, and my knee doesn't buckle the way it sometimes does first thing in the morning. A few careful movements bring some pain, but my mobility is already better than it was.

Maybe he wasn't shitting me after all.

The thought rocks me back on my heels. *This*, out of every-thing, doesn't make sense. I'm here. I'm more or less willing to play my part. I might hold out as long as possible, but it's inevitable I end up in his bed at some point. Especially with that bite of his. He has absolutely no reason to heal me. None. Not when I've already admitted my father pulverized my knee because I have a history of running.

I don't understand this vampire, and that scares me more than anything else that's happened.

I make a circuit around the room. My suitcase is gone, which initially fills me with panic, but I find it tucked in the wardrobe, along with all my clothing, which has been unpacked. I frown at the neat row of shirts and pants and dresses. "Pushy."

The thought of putting clean clothes on without cleaning my body first makes me leave the wardrobe and go check the second door I didn't bother with this morning. Sure enough, it leads to a bathroom. I don't have high hopes for the plumbing, but when I turn the faucet on the large copper tub, the water comes out clear and hot.

I eye the door. I could try to block it, but what's the point? If he really wants into the room, he'll end up here, chair in front of the doorknob or no.

Will he see me *not* locking the door as an invitation?

I refuse to examine that thought too closely as I strip and step into the tub. The water is hot enough to make me hiss out a surprised breath, but I sink down into it all the same and lean my head back. I didn't realize how cold I was until now, when heat begins soaking into my body.

The creak of a floorboard has me opening my eyes to find Malachi leaning against the wall across from the tub. I narrow my eyes. "Did you make a sound on purpose?"

"You seem opposed to me surprising you."

"Gee, I wonder why?"

He crosses his arms over his chest, which leads me to realize he's changed since I saw him last, too. Now he's wearing a pair of low-slung pants...and nothing else. His body is too lean for his wide shoulders and sturdy frame, confirming my suspicion he's gone without regular feedings for a long time. And he's covered in scars. The one over his heart is the worst of them, but there are slashing and stabbing marks and more than a few bullet holes. And that's just what I can see from my position.

I frown. "If your healing power is so superior, why are you scarred up?"

"I'm surprised you don't know. If the wound is made with silver, it doesn't always heal properly." He touches the one over his heart. "The scarring is mostly surface-level, though."

I *hadn't* known that. Why didn't I know that?

I study him. "Are you here to collect your daily feeding?"

"You don't seem particularly opposed to the idea."

No, opposed isn't the word I'd use. Damn it, but even the sight of him has desire coursing through me. There's no point in denying it, either, because his senses are acute enough to pick up on all the signs. "Might as well get it over with."

Malachi's lips curve. "Such a noble sacrifice."

"You're stronger than me. Faster than me. And your bite ensures I become a willing victim the second you get your fangs into my skin. Fighting you is pointless, and I try to save my strength for battles I can win." It sounds logical enough, even if I feel anything but.

The bastard laughs. It's just as rusty as the last time. "No, Mina. I'm not here to take my *daily feeding*."

I draw my knees to my chest and refuse to categorize the sinking feeling inside me. "Then why *are* you here?"

"I suppose I owe you an apology." He studies me for a long moment. "All the others who've come through that door felt differently about the role than you do. If I hadn't been half-starved, I would have realized it."

Half-starved. *I knew it.* "Why wait for your meal to come to you? You're more than capable of taking care of it yourself."

He ignores the question and taps his fingers against his forearm. "I suppose if you want your freedom, you're more than welcome to leave."

Ah, so this is just another game. I glare. "You should really work on your sense of humor. You know as well as I do I can't leave."

"Do I?" He doesn't move. "Walk out the door. I won't stop you."

"And the guards my father has posted around the property?"

His mouth tightens. "I'll handle it. I'm more than capable of keeping them distracted long enough for you to slip away."

For a moment, I almost believe him. Freedom is what I crave more than anything else in the world. If there's a chance...

But then reality raises its ugly head.

I have nowhere to go. No money. No way to pass among the humans without raising some eyebrows and doing something that puts me on the government's radar. From there, it's a short trip to a padded cell, at best. At worst, to some scientist's lab to be experimented on for the rest of my life. With enough preparation, I might be able to slip into the world without a ripple, but I don't have that knowledge or the resources required.

Not to mention the fact that my father will not let me leave in peace. If he realizes I've run, he'll send his hunters after me. There's nowhere I can hide they won't find me, and when they drag me right back, I'll be worse off than I started.

No. No matter how much I dream of running, it's not really an option. It never was.

I close my eyes and fight against the burning behind my lids.

I don't know if he's doing this on purpose, but it feels particularly cruel to offer me what I've always wanted and force me to reject it. "I'm staying."

"The offer stands."

I press my lips together, hating the way the bottom one quivers. My anger feels so far away right now. *Everything* feels far away right now. "You are such a bastard."

"I've been accused of worse."

I finally look at him again. Desperate to focus on something else, I go back over what he said. How he apologized. How he dodged my one question. Why he'd be so starved even though he seems more than capable enough of hunting. I frown. "You're stuck here, too, aren't you?"

Malachi lifts a single shoulder. "It's complicated."

Complicated. Smells like vampire politics to me.

I push it away. It's a mystery for another day, and I'm suddenly too exhausted to poke at him any longer. "I suppose we might as well fuck since you've rubbed my nose in the fact that I'm stuck here."

He barks out a laugh. "Enjoy the rest of your bath, little dhampir." A blur of movement and he's gone, the door closing softly behind him.

Every time I think I've managed my expectations, he does something to pull the rug out from beneath my feet. I don't understand what's going on, and I don't feel like things are going to change any time soon.

It takes three minutes to acknowledge the relaxation of my bath is ruined. I wash quickly and get out. After some consideration, I pull on a pair of yoga pants and a baggy shirt before I leave the room. I need food.

And maybe part of me wants to provoke another encounter with Malachi. He's so unexpected, I never quite know what he'll do. Attack. Seduce. Apologize. He's brought my most unforgivable trait to the fore.

He's made me curious.

I make my way back to the kitchen and stop short in the doorway. It almost looks like a different room from the one I visited earlier. Every surface gleams and it smells faintly of lemon. The only thing that remains from yesterday is the faded paint of the walls. I walk to the fridge and pull it open, my jaw dropping at the sight of it filled to capacity with a wide variety of food and drink. "What the hell?"

I slept through the majority of the day, and I expected Malachi did the same. Sunlight is barely an inconvenience for vampires, no matter what the human legends say, but most of them prefer to keep nocturnal schedules to avoid the irritating brightness. Either there's someone else in the house with us... Or he cleaned the kitchen and stocked the fridge for me.

How the hell did he stock the fridge if he's trapped here?

"Tricky vampire," I murmur. I shove down the weird warmth in my chest. Of course he's ensuring I can feed myself. I'm no use to him if I starve to death, and no matter how much power his blood carries, I still need actual food to survive. The blood bank dries up if I die. Surely that's why he did this. Believing anything else is a fool's thought.

Refusing to eat out of spite is silly, so I grab the makings for a light breakfast that's heavy in protein. It feels strange to sit at the kitchen table and eat slowly rather than shove food in my mouth before someone decides to deprive me. My father always allowed me meals in a begrudging manner, as if my very need to eat inconvenienced him. It didn't seem to matter there were other humans in the colony who had the same biological requirements I do. Every reminder of my human side irritated him.

At least until he found a use for me.

I blink down at my empty plate. I'm not sure how long I've been staring at it. I give myself a shake and clean up my dishes and put everything away. I look around the kitchen again and frown. What am I supposed to *do* for all the hours in between Malachi biting me? In the colony, after breakfast, I'd immediately be put to work at whatever menial task I was assigned that day. Before my knee injury, I'd sneak in a workout at some point, too. The younger turned vampires loved to spar with me because it gave them an excuse to beat the shit out of me. They'll always be faster, but I picked up plenty of skills in the process.

With nothing else to do, I go exploring. The house is more or less what I expect. Room after room on the verge of decay, all with peeling wallpaper or fading paint. Dust covering everything. The whole house needs an update in the worst way.

I stop at the back door and stare out over the fields behind the house. A ring of trees mask the fence I know circles the entire property, a tall imposing iron monstrosity designed to deter even the most curious explorer. I'm reasonably sure I can wander anywhere within that fence without worrying about running into the guards, but I'm not willing to test it out. Not yet.

Instead, I turn around and head upstairs. More rooms, most of them bedrooms, but I hit the jackpot in the back corner of the house. I walk through the door and have the strangest feeling I've walked into a different building entirely. It's been converted to a passably modern gym. The walls are painted a new-ish white and the dusty carpet has been torn up and replaced with wood floors that are only moderately beat up. A free-weight set looms in the back corner, stacks upon stacks of weights on the bar. A fancy treadmill is pushed against the other wall, angled to look out the window. In the center is a mat similar to what we had in the colony for sparring.

Huh.

I poke at the treadmill, a bittersweet feeling rising in my chest. There was a time when I would have given my left arm to have access to equipment like this. A chance to properly *train*. My knee might feel okay right now, but I suspect it's a false feeling created as a side effect from taking Malachi's blood. No matter what he seems to think, even vampire blood can't fix something already healed. He'd have to rebreak my knee, and even then I doubt there's enough structure left to ensure it'd heal properly the second time. No, he's simply acting the way all vampires do naturally—with casual cruelty.

My neck prickles and I speak without turning around. "I thought you weren't going to sneak up on me anymore."

"It's not my fault your dhampir senses aren't acute enough to hear me coming, even when I'm not trying to mask my steps."

I turn to find Malachi's changed again. He's wearing a pair of loose pants, and he's foregone a shirt again. He's even tied back his long hair. Obviously, he's here to work out. I clear my throat. "Don't let me interrupt you. I was just checking out the house." I hesitate. "Um, thank you for the food. And for cleaning the kitchen so I can actually make it without worrying about giving myself some kind of lead poisoning or some shit from whatever old paint is on the walls."

He moves a few steps into the room. "Would you like to spar, little dhampir?"

5

I BLINK. HE WANTS TO *SPAR?* "WHAT?"

"It would be useful to see your skill level."

His words are logical, but that doesn't mean they make sense. "Why do you care what my *skill level* is? I'm only here for two reasons." Maybe that's what his offer is about. A reminder of my place here. I'm not foolish enough to nourish the false hope he's different from every single vampire I've ever known. The odds of that are astronomically not in my favor.

"Indulge me." The steel in his tone informs me this is less a suggestion than a command.

I could try to push back, but it'd just end in us sparring while I attempt to escape the room. The thought of him getting his hands on me again has my traitorous heartbeat kicking up a notch. "You just want to bite me again."

"If I want to bite you, I'll bite you." He moves closer, backing me onto the mat. "Surely your father didn't leave you completely defenseless. Show me what you can do."

I snort. "You have a heightened opinion of my father he doesn't deserve."

He clenches his jaw. "Trust me. He deserves everything I think of him."

Not sure what I'm supposed to say to *that*, but it doesn't matter because he strikes. He slows himself down enough that I can see him coming—but only barely. I jerk back, and I can actually feel the air displacement against my cheek where his fist moves. "What the hell?"

"Stop arguing and spar, Mina."

I try for a right jab, but he shifts out of the way. He's fast, and it feels like I'm moving through water by comparison. "Even a dhampir can't hold their own in a fight against a vampire."

"Sounds like an excuse to me." He hits me in the stomach. It's barely strong enough to knock me back a step. "Again."

I glare. "This is pointless."

Malachi arches a brow. "Is it? I already know plenty about you." When I glare, he jerks his chin at my body. "Your form is abysmal, you have no formal training, and you favor your injured knee even though it's not bothering you as much as it did yesterday."

I drop my hands. "Like I said, this is pointless."

"Are you going to flee from every single confrontation, Mina?" The question is quiet and strangely serious. "Are you so sure you know everything there is to know about the world at...what? Twenty-five years old? Can you truthfully say there's nothing left to learn?"

I open my mouth to argue but stop myself before any of the angry words can escape. It's like he's found a wound I didn't know existed and he's digging his fingers around in it. Finally, I say, "Why do you care?"

"You have potential."

That isn't an answer. Not really. "What does that mean?"

"There was a time when dhampirs were far more common than they are now. I don't know what your fool of a father told you, but you haven't begun to reach your upper limits." He's watching me closely, each word a precision missile aimed at the heart of me. "With proper nutrition and a steady diet of vampire blood, you'll be easily as strong and fast as a turned vampire. Possibly as a born vampire, albeit without the magical abilities."

"Don't lie to me." I sound too harsh, but I don't care. What he's saying... I know all too well how hope can become a weapon used to break an opponent. That has to be what Malachi is doing right now. It *must* be. "I know my role in all this. You don't have to be cruel."

He watches me for a long moment. "Give me a chance to convince you."

"*Why?* Even if what you're saying is true, why would you want me stronger? Then I could fight you off, possibly even kill you."

His lips curve. "I have my reasons."

Reasons that no doubt include tormenting me. I shake my head. "No. You get to fuck with my blood and my body. You don't get to fuck with my head."

"And if I offer you a bargain?"

It feels like my feet have sprouted roots, each one holding me in place when I just want to run away from this vampire and this conversation. But then, what would be the point? Even without my knee injury, he's faster than me. He'll *always* be faster than me. I swallow hard. "What bargain?"

"Train with me. Exchange blood. As long as you're doing that, sex is off the table."

I stare. "You're lying."

"I think you'll find, Mina, I never lie." He shrugs a single shoulder. "Sometimes I withhold the truth, but I give you my word I won't fuck you while you're meeting your end of the bargain." He flashes me a hint of fang. "Unless you ask nicely."

"It'll never happen," I shoot back, even as part of me wonders. I can't deny I want him, whether it's bite-induced lust or pure lust. He's gorgeous and strong and there's a sly intelligence in those dark eyes that draws me despite myself. I can't blame all that on his intoxicating bite, no matter how much I'd like to.

"Then you have no reason to say no to the bargain."

It's too good a deal. Why would he offer this? I frown. "Every time you bite me, I orgasm."

"I can't control that."

"And if I beg you to fuck me while I'm all drugged up on your bite?"

Another of those quick flashes of fangs. "I won't fuck you until you ask me nicely while my fangs aren't inside you."

I don't know if I believe him, but I'd be a fool not to take this bargain. What if he's *not* lying? "You have yourself a deal."

"Then we can begin."

I don't know what I expected, but Malachi immediately begins correcting my stance and then we proceed to spar in slow motion while he critiques me. I had thought I'd learned something in the colony, but with every word, he flays my confidence down to nothing at all. After an hour of it, he stands back. "That's enough for today."

I'm covered in sweat and shaking like a leaf. I'm not sure I have the strength to make the trip to my bedroom, but I'll be damned before I admit as much.

Malachi stalks to a low stool set against one wall and motions me closer with an impatient flick of his fingers. I tense. I know what comes next. The biting. "Why can't we do it standing?"

"Because you're going to collapse again and I have no interest in accidentally ripping your throat out."

My face flames. My embarrassment is made more overwhelming by the fact that he's right. I can't seem to control my body when he bites me. I pad to him slowly and don't argue when he takes my hand and pulls me down to straddle him on the stool. He runs a broad hand up my back to fist in my hair and tow my head gently to the side. I don't have a chance to brace myself before he strikes, sinking his fangs into me.

Gods, it's so good.

I clutch his shoulders and relax against him. His strength will hold me up, keep me caged, and I can't decide if it's a good thing or a bad thing. Why am I fighting this? It feels so good, it's hard to remember my reasons.

Each pull feels like he's stroking my breasts, my clit, my pussy.

His free hand lands on the small of my back, urging me closer, and I'm only too eager to obey the silent command. I *need*. I roll my hips, rocking against his hardening cock. It feels so good. Too good. If Malachi stripped us and bore me to the floor, I'd welcome him happily. Knowing that, somehow trusting he won't… It makes me bolder. I dig my fingers into his hair and moan.

Malachi growls against my skin, but instead of sucking harder, he lifts his head and drags his tongue over the spot where he bit me. "You taste too fucking good. I don't understand it."

"Keep going."

"No." He leans back, easily overpowering my hold, and reaches up to grab my chin. He runs his thumb over my bottom lip, urging my mouth open, and presses the pad of his thumb against one of my canine teeth. They're a little more prominent than a human's but nowhere near as long as a vampire's. He frowns. "I don't think you can break skin effectively with these little things."

"Wow, I didn't realize you were a size queen."

His grin is quick and nearly knocks me on my ass. "We'll have to improvise." As I watch, he drags his tongue over his tooth, cutting it. Malachi shifts his grip to the back of my neck. "Come here."

He doesn't even have to pull me. I'm already moving, diving down and taking his mouth. He tastes of blood and man and, *gods*, I can't get enough. I wish I could say it's because of the blood zinging across my tongue and setting fire to my veins as if he's poured lightning down my throat. That would be less unforgivable than the truth.

I like kissing Malachi.

He holds me easily to him and plunders my mouth. Tongue and teeth clash, this moment as much a battle as our earlier sparring. Maybe I shouldn't like that. Maybe I should crave a softer touch, something like my single kiss before this. A tentative brush of lips against mine. A stolen moment filled with yearning. At least on my side... At least until I realized Darrien only kissed me on a dare from his friends.

That slams me out of this moment. No matter how devastating this kiss is, Malachi isn't kissing me because he's so overcome with lust he had to have my mouth on his. No, he's playing a game of chess and I'm already seven moves behind.

I force myself to lift my head. It's only then I realize I can't taste his blood any longer. He healed while we were kissing. If I hadn't pulled away, would he have stopped me on his own? I look down into his handsome face, his eyes violently dark with desire, and I just don't know.

I lick my lips, tasting him there. "That's enough."

"As long as you're satisfied." His voice is as rough as I feel. He strokes the small of my back, the slightest touch that almost seems to urge me to keep riding him.

I want to demand he bite me again, do the one thing guaranteed to override my spiraling thoughts long enough for me to orgasm like this. Worse, I almost don't care if the bite is even involved. I want him to keep touching me, to keep doing this until neither of us can think anymore.

That's the problem, though. *I* might lose myself, but Malachi won't. I can almost guarantee it. Aside from that first time in the foyer, he's been perfectly in control during every encounter. Unlike me.

I shove to my feet and nearly land on my ass. For once, Malachi doesn't move to catch me, merely watching as I stumble back until I'm steady. I press my fingers to my lips. "Give me the knife back and you won't have to *improvise* again."

He smiles, flashing a little fang. "No."

"So this is all a trap. You say you aren't going to sleep with me and then you cross lines all over the place the first chance you get." I'm trying to work up a good mad, but my body is still crying out from the loss of his. I *ache* in a way I'm terrified only he can fix.

"Don't be naive, Mina. A kiss is not the same thing as sex." He leans forward and props his forearms on his knees. The position should look relaxed, but every one of my prey instincts is screaming he's half a second from pouncing on me. "When I fuck you, it won't be with a little tongue." Another of those slow smiles. "But if you're feeling needy and want me to kiss your pussy better, I'm more than happy to."

I take a measured step back. Now is the time to retreat, to take the out he's offered me and put some distance between us. It's what a smart woman would do in my position. But then, a smart woman would have run the second she had the chance and damned the consequences. I'm here. For better or worse, I'm choosing this. I lick my lips. "Prove it."

6

THE WORDS BARELY LEAVE MY MOUTH BEFORE HE'S ON
me, bearing me to the ground. Once again, he makes a cage of
his body and protects me from any impact. Malachi takes my
mouth in a rough kiss. His fangs nick my tongue. Or maybe it's
his tongue. Hell, maybe it's both. All I know is I taste blood and
add a bolt of sheer lust to what's already a tidal wave of desire.

He's already moving down my body before I have a chance
to sink into the sensation, kissing my breasts through my thin
shirt before he settles between my thighs. I prop myself up on my
elbows, breathless and a little shocked. "Um."

He trails his finger down the seam of my yoga pants, stopping directly over my clit. "Changed your mind?"

"No." The word bursts out before I can think about the intelligence of waving a red flag in front of a bull.

"Good." He does something, moving too quickly for me to follow. One second we're staring at each other and the next he's ripped my pants in half. The movement jerks my hips closer to him and then his mouth is on me.

I tense, expecting a bite. *Anticipating* a bite. But instead of the sharp pleasure of his fangs, it's the soft heat of his tongue. He licks a long line up the center of my body. It feels so wrong and so right at the same time. His growl vibrates through my pussy and my arms give out. "*Fuck.*"

That's when he moves up to drag the tip of his tongue over my clit. Over and over again. I thought this would feel different from when he bites me, and it does... But not as different as I expected. It's too good. Desire drugs me, molten and fluid, winding tighter and tighter through my body.

I don't make a conscious decision to move. One second I'm trying to get my equilibrium back and the next my hands are in his hair, pulling him closer even as I lift my hips to grind against his mouth. "Oh gods, that feels so good."

He makes another of those hungry noises and then his tongue is inside me. He spears me with it, and the intrusion has me crying out in surprise. Malachi withdraws a little and lifts his head to look at me with eyes gone dark and feral. For a second, I could swear I see flames licking in their depths, but I blink and the illusion disappears. He drags his thumbs down either side of my pussy. "Mina." My name sounds like a sin on his lips.

I have to swallow hard before I can speak. "Yes?"

"Are you a virgin?"

I really, really don't want to answer that question. It's too loaded, too filled with implications I want nothing to do with. Vampire culture doesn't place the same importance on virginity as human culture does—at least according to the media I've consumed—but it remains a *thing*.

He watches me closely. "Answer me."

"Yes." The word feels dragged from my lips against my will.

Malachi presses his forehead to my lower stomach for a long moment. "Okay." He exhales harshly. "Okay."

I don't know what he means. I just know I might die if he leaves me on this ledge. "Please."

"Give me a second."

Give *him* a second? What the hell kind of game is he playing right now?

My breath sobs from my throat. "Malachi." I dig my fingers into his hair, but I'm not strong enough to move him on my own. "Malachi, *please*."

He hesitates and then his mouth is back at my pussy. He picks up right where he left off, spearing me with his tongue and then moving back to my clit. Each little circle he makes ratchets my need higher. He has to pin my hips in place to keep me from writhing too far from his tongue.

Between one gasp and the next, I orgasm. I cry out, the wave crashing over me strongly enough to leave me breathless. It feels so good, so incredibly good, just as good as his bite but at the same time better. And then he bites me and I lose my fucking mind.

I think I might be screaming. I can't tell. All I know is I manage to haul him up my body or maybe he's already moving up on his own. He claims my mouth and then he's between my thighs and thrusting, grinding his cock against my pussy, his thin pants the only thing keeping us from fucking.

I want them out of the way. I want him inside me. I *want.*

I open my mouth to tell him, but his tongue is there, stealing my words, my thoughts, my very sanity. One of us is snarling. It might be me. I can't stop, rolling my body up to meet his every stroke. I taste myself and blood on his tongue, and it only drives my frenzy higher. *More, more, more. Don't stop.*

I come again and he goes still against me. He lifts his head and this time I know I'm not imagining the flames in his eyes. I'm breathing so hard, I'm gasping. "Malachi?"

He strokes a hand down my thigh, hitching my leg up around his waist. His pants are wet, but I can't tell if it's because of me or because of him. He drops his head to my neck and keeps moving against me, rocking in an almost decadent motion. I cling to him, barely managing to keep from begging him to fuck me.

The first sign something's gone wrong is the heat flickering against my arm.

I open my eyes and shriek. "*Fire.*"

Malachi doesn't stop moving against me. He doesn't seem to notice the flames licking at the floorboards in almost a perfect circle around us. It's not getting closer, but *the room is on fire.* I yank on his hair. "Malachi." Still no response.

In a panic, I do the only thing I can think of. I squirm my hand between our bodies and grab his cock in a ruthless grip. He rears back, his eyes entirely black. Smoke burns my throat. "*Fire, Malachi.*"

He blinks and gives himself a shake. A brief wave of his hand and the flames smother themselves. "Sorry."

I stare at the burned floor. I know all seven of the bloodlines have different magical properties associated with them, but my father decided I didn't need to know more than that. He never saw fit to inform me that Malachi's is *fire*. I swallow hard, tasting ash. "Is that going to happen every time we make out?"

He slumps on top of me and gives a hoarse laugh. "No. I lost control."

That's not nearly as comforting as he seems to think it is. "Let me get this straight. We didn't even have sex and you lost control enough to set the room on fire."

He still seems to have no desire to move off me. "Your blood is intoxicating, little dhampir. It's easy to lose myself in you."

I blink at the ceiling. "So it's *my* fault you lost control and almost killed us both?"

"No." He finally sits back and pulls me up with him. "It's simply the way things are. But you were never in any danger. I wouldn't have let the fire touch you."

There *is* a perfect circle around us of untouched floor. "I can die from smoke inhalation. Or the floor could have collapsed and given us both an inconvenient stake in the heart. So yeah, I think I might have been in some danger."

He frowns at the charred boards as if he never considered those outcomes. But then, why would he? No matter that he keeps calling me dhampir, he keeps drinking my blood, he seems to forget sometimes I'm not operating on the same level he is. I think it might be a compliment if it wasn't likely to get me killed on accident.

Finally Malachi shakes his head. "It won't happen again."

"But—"

"It won't happen again," he repeats firmly.

Maybe I should let this go, but I can't quite manage it. "You've drank my blood several times in the last couple days and this hasn't happened before." He also wasn't licking an orgasm out of me before now, either, but surely *that* isn't enough to undermine his control so thoroughly. I have never heard of a vampire losing it like this during sex, let alone foreplay. Granted, my information is incomplete, but surely people would talk about it if it was a real risk? Vampires might be immortal, but that doesn't mean they can't be killed. Any of the seven bloodlines have powers strong enough to kill. If they lose it every time someone orgasms, their lines all would have died out a long time ago.

Malachi sits back on his heels and drags his hand over his face. "I underestimated the strength of your blood. It's increased my strength as a result."

I pull my legs to my chest, acutely aware my yoga pants no longer cover the essentials. "I thought you've drank from dhampirs before. Why didn't you expect this?"

"Because none of the dhampirs I've tasted before had this effect on me." His dark gaze turns contemplative, and I notice his pupils have retreated to their customary shape, no longer bleeding over the entirety of his eyes. "It's strange."

When it comes to vampires, *strange* is not an asset. Something akin to panic bleats through my veins. "Stop it."

"What?"

"I don't know what game you're playing, but stop it. I am not special and I am not a mystery and I'm not any of the other shit you're about to spout." It *has* to be a game. It's the only thing that makes sense. Rejecting his musings is the only thing that will keep me sane. The mystery he paints is too tempting by half.

Everyone wants to be special. To be unique. Me more than most. When you're a dhampir, especially one without a lick of magic to speak of, you can never measure up no matter what you do. Never strong enough, fast enough, just flat-out never *enough*. Malachi acting like this is just cruel. "Don't you think if my blood was some kind of magical booster, someone would have figured it out by now?"

His expression is painfully serious. "Have many vampires fed from you more than once?"

A fair question, but it stings all the same. "No. Of course not. I think my father had me destined as a sacrifice from the moment I was born, so he didn't exactly pass me around to his people." I look away. "I've been bit a couple times during sparring." And a couple times outside it. "But it was rare."

"By turned vampires."

"Yes."

"Then how would you know if your blood boosts a bloodline's power?"

I open my mouth but close it without answering. Again, a fair question. It doesn't make it less cruel. "I am not special."

He frowns. "Yes, Mina. You are. Even without the blood element."

That's about enough of that.

I shove to my feet and start for the door. I barely make it one step before Malachi sweeps me into his arms. He glares at my sound of protest. "You'll burn your feet."

"I just drank a bunch of your blood. I'll heal."

"All the same." Except he doesn't set me down once we're out of the room. He just keeps moving at that dizzying pace until we arrive back at my room. Malachi pauses in the doorway and sets me on my feet. He frowns at the bed. "I'll order new things for the room."

That startles a laugh out of me. "Oh, you're just now remembering maybe I don't want to sleep in a dusty old bed? Lovely."

He gives me a long look. "Are you angry about the fire or something else?"

It's so, so tempting to confess what has me twisted in knots, but if I honestly believe he's playing games with my mind, then telling him what I'm feeling is just opening a path for him to fuck with me further. I can't risk it. "I'm tired. Good night, Malachi." I shut the door in his face.

Even so, I clearly hear him through the thick wood. "I am not the enemy."

I want to believe him. I want it so badly I can taste it like the coppery tang of blood on my tongue. But there's one lesson my father taught me, one I cannot afford to forget. Not even with Malachi. Especially not with him.

Everyone is the enemy.

7

THE REST OF THE WEEK FALLS INTO AN INCREASINGLY familiar pattern. I wake up, wander down to the newly shiny kitchen for a meal and coffee, and then explore the house. At some point, Malachi shows up and drags me to spar and train. When I'm shaking with fatigue, he bites me. I always orgasm. I always bite him back.

But he doesn't kiss me or offer to *kiss it better* again.

Even as I tell myself to be grateful, my irritability rises with each passing day. I want him and I don't want to want him, and it was easier to live in my head when I told myself I didn't have a choice. Malachi is effectively undermining that narrative, and I'm not in the mood to be grateful. More, I'm mad at myself. I shouldn't want this. I shouldn't want *him*. Desiring Malachi is just playing into my father's plans, which is the last thing I want.

I'm so distracted by my tumultuous thoughts, I don't realize I'm not alone in the library for a moment too long. I catch sight of the blond vampire and jump off the couch I was sitting on, but I barely make it a step before he's on me. He digs his fingers into my hair and shoves me back onto the couch, following me down. He gets a knee between my thighs and grins at me. "What a delicious little thing you are."

Fear clamors in my throat, but I refuse to show it to this stranger. "I don't know who you are, but you have five seconds to get off me or I'm going to cut your fucking head off."

"So vicious." He says it slowly, like he's savoring it. "I like it."

In the flickering light of the fire, his features seem exaggerated. High cheekbones. Hollow cheeks. Freakishly pale eyes that still seem encased in shadows. His blond hair is cut into a short mohawk, and though he's smaller than Malachi, he's still stronger than me.

I am so fucking *tired* of everyone else being stronger than me.

"Who the hell are you?"

His grin is a little deranged, flashing fang. "You can call me Wolf."

Wolf. The name tingles a memory, but I can't quite grasp it. Not when I'm in immediate danger of getting my throat ripped out. He's not one of my father's, though. I know that much. Which means he's a wild card and I can't anticipate what the hell he's going to do.

Except bite me.

That's all but guaranteed with the way he's watching my pulse thrum beneath my skin. "Malachi will kill you."

"Nah." He laughs. "We're old friends." Wolf raises his voice. "Aren't we, Malachi?"

"Wolf." I didn't see Malachi enter the room, but then I've been more than a little distracted. I turn my head as much as I'm able and find him standing a few feet away, his hands casually tucked into his pockets as if he's not witnessing a trespasser pinning me to the couch. "It's been a long time."

"Your choice. Not mine." Wolf transfers my wrists to one hand and turns to keep Malachi in his line of vision. "Imagine my surprise to find you're accepting sacrifices from that jackal Cornelius again. Tsk, tsk, Malachi. No one likes a hypocrite."

"Extenuating circumstances." Malachi's gaze flicks to me. "You have something of mine."

Wolf laughs again. The sound is downright sinful. It sounds like good chocolate tastes, decadent and a little bittersweet. "You've been alone too long, my friend. You've gotten greedy and forgotten how to be a good host." He licks his lips. "I'm positively *parched*."

Malachi hesitates for a long moment, and a traitorous hope whispers to life in my chest. Surely he won't let this stranger bite me. Surely he can see how much I am not on board with this idea. Surely...

"Help yourself." He drops into the chair across from us. "Biting only."

Wolf looks back at me, and the cruelty in his pale eyes is matched only by the amusement lingering there. "Did you think he'd step in? Poor thing, you've really done a number on her, Malachi."

"Wolf." The warning in Malachi's tone seems not to register.

Wolf runs a single finger down my neck. His eyes flick to mine, and his grin softens the tiniest bit. "Don't worry, love. It'll feel good."

Which means he's a bloodline vampire, too. I don't care. "A chemical reaction. That doesn't mean a single damn thing. I don't want it."

He contemplates me, pointedly ignoring the way Malachi tenses in the chair at the edge of our vision. He inhales and goes still. "Ah. Not a human at all, are you? Dhampir." He settles down on top of me, using his body to keep me in place. He smells faintly spicy, like cloves and cinnamon or something similar. I hate that I don't hate it.

Wolf nuzzles my throat, and then his voice is in my ear, so low I can barely hear him. "Look how quickly he gave you away. Doesn't that make you angry? Do you see how still he sits? He doesn't want me to bite you, and yet he's not going to stop me. How does that make you feel?"

"Angry," I bite out.

"Thought so." His breath ghosts against the shell of my ear. "I'll do what he didn't. I'll ask permission. Let me bite you." He chuckles, low and decadent. "It'll piss him off something fierce."

He's trying to manipulate me, but even knowing that, it's working. I am *furious* at Malachi. Furious at myself for looking to him to be my savior when every other experience I've had with a vampire proves they can't be trusted. I forgot, and the sting of that knowledge is what prompts me to do something I never would have otherwise. "Do it."

"Wicked girl." He doesn't give me a chance to brace. He strikes, sinking his fangs into my throat. Instantly, pleasure pulses through me, heady and intense. Wolf's grip on my wrists keeps me from reaching for him, which is just as well. It doesn't stop me from arching against him and moaning. I'm angry enough that I don't try to fight it.

Malachi wants to give me to this vampire like a host offering a selection of wine? Well, he can damn well watch it happen.

I expect Wolf to pull something shady, but even as his cock hardens against me, he keeps his hands exactly where they started: one around my wrists and another braced next to my hip. The only move he makes is to stroke his thumb along the exposed skin at my side where my shirt has slid up during my struggle. It feels like he's touching me somewhere else. Or maybe that's the bite doing all the work for him, each pull as if he has his mouth all over my pussy.

I moan again. Distantly, I hear something crack, but I'm too invested in Wolf's bite to try to look. He presses a little more firmly between my thighs. Not quite a stroke, but it doesn't matter because it's enough to send me hurtling into orgasm. I come hard, panting out each breath. Distantly, I'm aware of him slipping his fangs from me and a little zing at my neck I can't identify. Then his tongue is there, cleaning the last of my blood from my skin.

Finally, a small eternity later, he releases me and sits up, flopping back against the other arm of the couch with a groan. "Malachi, you've been keeping secrets."

I turn my head, wondering at the lack of pain from the motion, and see that Malachi has completely demolished the arms of the chair where he's sitting. It looks like he exploded them; there's little more than kindling on the floor.

Petty satisfaction buoys me. There weren't good options in this scenario, but I chose this and I hope he fucking choked on the sight of Wolf on top of me. I ease up and lean against the other arm of the couch. My head is a little fuzzy from blood loss, but when I lift my hand to my neck, there are no wounds.

Wolf gives me a grin that's, well, wolfish. "You look surprised, love. Doesn't Malachi close the bite marks with his blood when he tastes you?"

"No." He lets me drink from him, which accelerates my healing. But I'm not in the mood to talk about this. I start to climb to my feet. "You are both assholes."

"Stay." The amusement disappears from Wolf's voice. "We have something to discuss and it involves you."

Even as I curse myself, I look at Malachi. He nods the tiniest amount. Not a command but a request. It doesn't change the fact that I'm pissed at him, but I relax back against the couch and pull my knees up. Wolf is still too close, and his spicy scent is all over me. It makes me want to simultaneously purr and scream, and I don't understand why I can smell him so intensely. He's not wearing any scent. There are no artificial tones in there that would signify perfume. But my nose has never been this sensitive before.

Wolf props his feet on the coffee table. I belatedly notice he's wearing a strange outfit. Fitted pants tucked into bulky black boots I suspect are steel-toed. A graphic T-shirt and a jacket that has a gothic feel to it complete the picture. He catches me looking and winks at me before turning his attention to Malachi. "You know the reason he sent her here instead of another one of those hapless humans is because he wants your bloodline."

Malachi doesn't move. "I'm aware."

"The second you knock her up, Cornelius is going to come collect his daughter, and then he'll have your child under his control—and as leverage."

It's exactly what my father has planned, but I can't help looking at Wolf more closely. He's given the impression of a vampire who's been around long enough to lose some of his sanity. Now he's lost the deranged tone and sounds nearly as serious as Malachi does normally. He taps his fingers on the arm of the couch. "You need to break the ward."

The ward?

What's he talking about?

I look at Malachi, but he's acting like I'm not in the room. He leans back against his chair as if the demolished remains of its arms aren't littering the floor at his feet. "Careful there, Wolf. One might start to think you care."

"That bastard having access to more bloodlines is bad news for all of us. His success with you has made him bold. He's hunting some of the others."

"You mean he's hunting you."

Wolf gives a blood-tinged smile. "He's trying. Unlike *some*, I haven't let honor get in the way of power."

I sit perfectly still, my mind racing to catch up and fill in the blanks. Some of it is easy enough. My father is responsible for Malachi being unable to leave. I'd wondered at that, but not as hard as I should have. Vampires are eccentric creatures under the best of circumstances. It seemed entirely within the realm of possibility that Malachi was more than happy to stay in this house and have his meals delivered to him. Yes, there was some starving in the intervening years, but it seems strangely logical to suffer that than try to step out into human society with all the technological upgrades they've made in the last generation. I suspect that's the main reason humans have driven vampires back, knowing about their existence or not.

Humans adapt and evolve. Constantly.

Vampires don't. Oh, they're capable of it, but it's harder for them because their very nature is as entrenched as their immortality. Or maybe all immortals face the same challenges of being unable to evolve. I don't know.

What Wolf is saying, though, contradicts my assumption. It sounds like my father trapped Malachi here with more than vampire guards to ensure he could take control of his bloodline. That he plans to do the same to the other bloodlines in danger of dying out.

Which means Malachi's as trapped as I am.

Surely not. Surely I'm misreading the situation. "If there's a ward, why not just burn your way out?"

Wolf's the one who answers. "That's not how wards work, especially not the ones your father uses." He says *father* like it's a curse. "He used a blood ward, and it would take a human sacrifice or a being more powerful than a vampire to break it."

Human sacrifice. Being more powerful than a vampire.

My mind is spinning, or maybe it's the room. I'm not certain. I'm not certain of anything anymore. "You killed the last woman he sent. Why not use her death to free yourself?"

Malachi makes a move that's almost a flinch. "I didn't kill her. She killed herself."

"What?"

Wolf stretches and yawns. "Blood wards won't hold me, which is the only reason that bastard hasn't managed to trap me yet."

If blood wards don't hold him, that means...

I thought I was afraid before. I really did. Now, I can barely breathe past the terror clogging my throat. Even if I was never officially taught about the bloodlines and which power goes with which or the members of the families still alive, I was taught *this*.

Seven bloodlines. Seven powers. The elementals: earth, air, water, fire. They're dangerous, can turn the very world around a person against them. But the other three? Body, blood, spirit. My father is the latter, and I've seen what he can do with glamour and illusion when he's angry. I've *felt* it, had my deepest, darkest fears dragged forth and shoved in my face. Had my very mind turned against me. If he can do that kind of damage with only the mind, what more can Wolf do with the blood?

I'm trapped in this house with two deadly predators, and right now they're both looking at me like I'm a tasty snack.

8

"I'M GOING TO BED." I PUSH TO MY FEET, BUT WOLF IS there before me, moving so fast, I have to scramble back to avoid running into his chest. I end up back on the sofa, staring up at him.

His pale eyes flicker red. "I don't think so."

"Wolf."

He takes a slow step toward me. "You are too careful, Malachi. This girl tastes sweet and feels sweeter, and it's playing with your head because you've been alone too long. She's a sweet *trap* and you damn well know it. Kill her and free yourself."

He's not joking now. He means every word. He won't lose sleep in killing me, and I don't know why that surprises me. Why *anything* surprises me anymore. "Wait—"

"Back the fuck off, Wolf." The flames in the fireplace crackle in a way that can only be described as menacing. "Now."

For a second, I think he won't do it. The red in his eyes edges into crimson and he looks downright feral for a moment. Just a moment, though. Between one blink and the next, he relaxes and grins down at me. "Ah well. Another time."

I can't move. I should fight, should scream, should do *something*, but it's all I can manage to draw in harsh inhale after harsh inhale. Malachi is dangerous, but even if I don't understand him, he's got some kind of reason for what he does. Wolf is a rabid dog, a chaotic gale-force wind that whips back and forth unexpectedly. Just when I think I might have a read on him, he turns around and tosses me off a cliff.

"Out." The quiet menace in Malachi's voice has goose bumps rising over my skin.

Wolf finally nods. "We'll talk more tomorrow." He turns and strides out of the room, moving at a human pace. I don't know why that's scarier than if he blurred away, but it is.

Between one blink and the next, Malachi is out of the chair and pulls me into his arms. "Mina."

"Get off me." I mean it to come out like a command, but it's a whispered plea. I can't stop shaking. What the fuck just happened? I don't understand what's going on, don't understand the players, don't even understand the game.

Instead of obeying, he scoops me into his arms and sits on the couch, tucking me into his lap. "I'm sorry."

"No, you're not. Stop saying that when you don't mean it." Oh gods, my voice sounds watery and my throat is burning. I will *not* cry in front of this vampire, will not expose yet another weakness in his presence. He already has me outmatched in every way measurable; I won't give him this, too.

But my body hasn't gotten the memo. Something hot and wet escapes the corner of my eye. I lower my head, and Malachi allows me that much, but he uses the opportunity to tuck me more firmly against his chest.

"I'm sorry," he repeats. "No one is going to kill you."

That draws a ragged laugh from me. I hardly sound like myself. "If not you, then Wolf. If not him, then my father will once I've played out my role." I thought I'd have more time, more opportunity to find a way out. I lied to myself about how out-matched I really am. There's no point in lying any longer. I am a pawn in other peoples' power games, destined to be moved from one side of the board to the other without any agency of my own.

Malachi's arms tighten around me. "I won't let it happen."

"What are you going to do? You're trapped by a blood ward, and the only way to get out is to kill me." There goes that laugh again. Gods, I sound deranged but I can't help it. "Checkmate."

"No." He strokes my head with a surprisingly gentle touch. "There's another way. I just haven't found it yet."

I want to believe him, but my life has taught me otherwise. There is no hero waiting in the wings to sweep in and save me. There is no convenient plot twist that will let the good guys win. The only thing that matters is power, and I have none. Even Malachi, a bloodline vampire, doesn't have enough to get out of this mess.

That's not the only thing weighing me down right now, though. I might be smarter if it was, if the only thing I cared about was getting out and being free. But there's a hurt deep inside, a betrayal I hate myself for feeling. "You gave me to him."

He tenses and then sighs. "It's complicated."

"It doesn't seem complicated from where I'm sitting. I thought..." But no. I can't put *that* foolishness into words. No matter how blurred the lines have begun to feel, the truth is Malachi is a predator and I am prey. He might insist on boundaries and bargains, but they're illusions. Just like with my father, he holds all the power and I hold none.

I try to straighten, but he keeps me pressed against him. I glare at his chest. "How far do *guest privileges* go? If Wolf gets an itch, should I expect him to show up in my room and fuck me? Since I'm a resource to be shared and all."

Malachi says something in a language I don't recognize, but the tone sounds like a curse. "*No.*"

"If you say so." I try to stop talking, but I can't seem to put the brakes on my mouth. The hurt and frustration and rage well up and morph into poison dripping from my lips. "Maybe I'll let him. Since you're not interested in sex, I might as well do it with someone else. Wolf's scary, but he's hot, and I'd hate to die a virgin."

The only warning I get is Malachi tensing beneath me. One second I'm cradled in his arms, and the next I'm straddling him and he's gripping my hips nearly hard enough to hurt. His eyes are edging toward black and I know enough now to recognize the flames they contain aren't the same ones reflected by the fire. It doesn't matter that I'm technically on top. I have no more control in this position than if he pinned me down onto the couch the way Wolf did earlier.

He glares up at me. "What the fuck part of me giving you

space to find your feet translates into that thick head of yours as I don't want to have sex with you?"

"*My* thick head? You're the one who laid down that ridiculous bargain!" I'm yelling and I don't give a fuck. "And yeah, I thought maybe you weren't a total monster but then Wolf shows up here like some kind of horny punk phantom and you're just like 'help yourself, my dhampir captive tastes really good.' It's bullshit. What am I supposed to think, Malachi? You don't fucking talk to me. We spar and we bite each other and that's all it's been for a week."

"A week," he grinds out through clenched teeth. "Seven fucking days. You spent your entire life under the thumb of Cornelius and then he shipped you off here where you're just as trapped. Forgive the fuck out of me if I wanted you to choose me instead of just going along with it because you had no other option."

I laugh in his face. "Choose you? What the hell are you even talking about? Choosing you means I get my heart broken in the bargain. The *best case* scenario is that you never manage to knock me up and I die of old age in a hundred years or so while you keep living forever in this house my father has trapped you in. I get wrinkled and gray and you stay exactly as you are now? Tell me how that's not just another kind of hell."

Something around his mouth softens. "You've thought about it."

"No, I haven't." It's not even a lie, not really. "But it's just how things are. I'm not that lucky. It's more likely to be a worst-case scenario and you know it. Either I get pregnant and my father comes to collect me, keeps me locked up long enough to have the baby, and then kills me, or I don't get pregnant and he decides he's tired of waiting and comes here and kills me. Do you understand what I'm saying, Malachi? No matter which way you look at this situation, I end up dead."

"I won't let that happen." The quiet confidence in his voice almost makes me believe him. Almost.

"Are you a god instead of a vampire?" I shake my head. "We're both trapped here. You should have told me the circumstances of your side of it."

He starts to speak and shakes his head. "You're right."

I blink. I didn't expect him to actually agree with me. "What?"

"You're right. I've played this all wrong." His grip softens on my hips and he nudges me closer to him, pressing us more firmly together. Impossible to ignore that his cock is rock hard. Apparently the regular feedings mean he doesn't have to bite me to get it up. I shiver.

Malachi dips his thumbs beneath my shirt and strokes my skin. "I should have been honest with you."

"Uh-huh." I lick my lips.

"Why don't we try some honesty right now?" He holds my gaze. "The reason I stopped doing anything but biting you is because I don't trust myself not to seduce you into having sex with me before you're ready. I fucking ache for you, Mina, but I want you to choose me because you want me. I don't want it to be coerced because you're out of your mind with bloodlust."

He said something to the same effect before, but part of me believed it was just another manipulation. It doesn't feel like that right now. I carefully set my hands on his chest. "And what about Wolf?"

Something like guilt flickers over his expression before he locks it down. "We're friends. Sometimes more."

Friends. Sometimes more.

The truth reaches out and slaps me in the face. "You want to share me for more than just blood."

He holds my gaze. "Wolf and I fuck, Mina. We have since we were teenagers."

I don't ask how long ago that was. The bloodlines have been dying out for a very long time. Malachi could be a hundred years old, or he could be five hundred. The gap between us already feels miles long without adding age to it.

I try to think, try to understand what he's saying and not saying. "So you're going to keep fucking Wolf, but you want to fuck me, too, and you'd be into me also fucking Wolf," I say slowly.

"More or less."

"I—"

"You don't need to say anything now." He releases me, and despite the fact that he's still pressed against me, I feel unmoored. "I just wanted to clarify where things stand."

"Are you going to fuck him tonight?" The question pops out before I can think too closely about why I want to know.

Malachi carefully lifts me and sets me back to my place on the couch. "That'll depend on what Wolf has to say when I talk to him later."

That wasn't a yes, but it wasn't a no, either. Something like jealousy flickers to life in my chest, even if it's a foolish emotion I have no right to. Malachi isn't mine. I didn't choose him. Even if I *did,* Wolf has a claim that precedes my birth, let alone this week.

It's too much. I don't know what to think, what to feel. "Oh."

He tucks a strand of my hair behind my ear. "No matter what Wolf acts like, he won't touch you without permission."

"Permission from you," I say bitterly.

Malachi snorts. "How quickly you forget *you* told him to bite you, little dhampir." When I open my mouth to protest, he beats me there. "It doesn't matter why you did it. The fact remains that you did, and so he bit you. If you hadn't, he would have backed off."

It seems to defy belief. "He had me pinned to the couch."

"Mmm." He looks at the fire. "It changes nothing. Wolf will manipulate if it suits his purposes, though, so if you don't want him to fuck you, be careful what you say when his fangs are inside you."

This conversation has taken too many strange turns for me to keep up. I study his profile. "And if I have sex with him?"

Malachi meets my gaze. "Someday, you'll believe I'm not your father. I have no desire to own you, Mina." His hand snakes out and he grasps my chin. "I simply want you."

"You don't even know me."

"I know enough."

I don't know why I'm so determined to push him, to shove my way through his carefully cool exterior, but I can't seem to stop. I lean into his grip on my chin. "And what happens if Wolf knocks me up, Malachi? If he gets there first because you're too busy being noble to take what you want?"

His eyes flare and I hear the fire hiss behind me. "Do you want me to fuck you, little dhampir? All you have to do is ask. All you've ever had to do is ask." He leans forward, easily holding me immobile. "But you *do* have to ask. We started things poorly, and I'm not interested in playing the part of marauding beast any longer. If we do this, it's because you're choosing it, not because I forced the issue. Until you're ready to admit that, it's not happening."

Damn him. That's exactly what I'm not quite ready to admit. No matter how much I hate it, it's easier to pretend I don't have a choice. How else am I supposed to hold on to my rage, the only thing that's kept me alive this long?

To avoid answering, I say, "You really were starving when I got here, weren't you?"

"Vampires can't starve to death."

No, they just turn into dried-out corpses without blood. It's one of my father's favorite ways to punish the vampires that cross him. When I was ten, he freed one that had been locked up for nearly a hundred years. I had nightmares for weeks. "Not to death, no, but you can starve."

Malachi looks away. "My condition is no excuse for attacking you."

Maybe not, but it creates a bridge of understanding I'm not sure I wanted. If Malachi is trapped here with a blood ward, he's entirely reliant on my father for blood. The last sacrifice was sent before I was born. Even if she lasted a few years, when I showed up, Malachi had gone without blood for at least twenty years. The fact that he had the restraint not to drink me dry, to try to prepare me for what was coming, is a little astounding when taken with that perspective.

He strokes my bottom lip with his thumb and drops his hand almost reluctantly. "Go to bed, Mina."

It's on the tip of my tongue to ask him to fuck me. I want it. I'd be lying to myself if I said I didn't. I might even like this vampire, though it seems impossible to wrap my mind around. But in the end, I can't speak the words that will unlock us from this stalemate.

I climb to my feet on shaky legs. "Good night, Malachi."

"Good night, Mina."

9

I CAN'T SLEEP. I SHOULD HAVE KNOWN IT WAS A LOST cause before even trying, but hope springs eternal. Even now. I can't stop thinking about all the new information this night brought, trying to puzzle through it to figure out what's true and what's manipulation. The possibility it might *all* be true is...

I don't know what to think.

Even though I know I should stay in the relative safety of my room, eventually my rushing thoughts demand movement. If I can just work off some of this frantically circling energy, then maybe something will make sense.

Or that's what I tell myself as I pad barefoot down the hallway. Dawn already lightens the horizon, another night having passed with us at a standstill. I press my forehead to the thick glass of the window and breathe slowly. The coolness does nothing to douse my thoughts, my feelings.

I want Malachi.

It takes *so much* to admit that truth to myself. I don't like it. It's inconvenient and messy, but it *is* the truth. I meant what I said before—there is no way for this thing between us to play out that doesn't end in heartbreak. It's an impossible situation.

But then, my entire life is an impossible situation. I've had no choice, no recourse, *nothing* that was mine and mine alone. Every single thing I've done is a reaction with the intent to survive.

What if I simply...said yes? Took what Malachi is offering? Took my chances with this small slice of pleasure?

I lift my head and sigh. I'm looking for an excuse to fuck him. Maybe I just need to stop trying to reason my way through it and simply *do* it.

I don't make the decision to head for the stairs. My body simply moves on its own, each step taking me closer to Malachi's bedroom on the third floor. Am I really going to do this? I don't know. I just don't know.

A sound cuts through my inner turmoil. A soft grunt. I stop short. It almost sounds like someone's in pain, but even without much personal experience with it, I know what fucking sounds like. I should turn around. Should take the humiliation heating my cheeks and let it increase the distance between me and Malachi's room.

I don't. I walk down the hallway. The door is cracked, which feels almost like an invitation to press two fingers to the thick wood and push it open a few inches more. Just enough to see his bed. Just enough to see what he's doing to Wolf in it.

My breath stalls in my chest and my feet sprout roots to hold me in place. Both men are naked. Wolf is on his hands and knees, each muscle in his lean body looking carved from stone as he shoves himself back against Malachi. No. That's not what he's doing. He's shoving himself back onto Malachi's cock.

And Malachi?

Gods, he's a masterpiece. His thick hair is flung over one shoulder and his big body is one hard line, his ass flexing with each thrust as he takes Wolf's ass. It's brutal and they both look angry, as if they started a fight and ended up fucking despite themselves.

I should leave. Should walk away. Should do anything but stand here and watch like the worst kind of voyeur.

I wait for hurt or betrayal to rise, but there's nothing. He told me, after all. He and Wolf are friends who are sometimes more. No matter what Malachi wants from me, he obviously wants Wolf, too. I don't understand their history, don't really get how they can be so antagonistic and still seem to care about each other.

Wolf turns his head and meets my gaze. His eyes are the same crimson they were in the library and he grins, flashing fang. He opens his mouth, but I don't wait around to hear whatever he's about to say.

I turn and flee.

Each step brings a recrimination with it. Coward. Fool. Weakling. I say I want Malachi, but then the second I get the hint of an invitation to join in and I'm fleeing like a scared little girl.

I stop short at the top of the stairs. What am I doing? I make a decision and then instantly backtrack? Is that really what I'm made of? I close my eyes and take several deep breaths. I'll just talk to Malachi about it tomorrow like a reasonable person. That's a logical way to proceed. A nice easy pace.

"What a little coward you are."

I startle and start to tip down the stairs. My stomach goes weightless and I start to curl in on myself to minimize the damage I'm about to receive.

Rough hands grab my upper arms and yank me back to the relative safety of the third floor landing. Back against a naked chest. I don't have to look to know it's Wolf. He's shorter and leaner than Malachi. And even after only one encounter with him, I recognize the casual cruelty in the amused tone of his voice.

"Let me go."

"Is that any way to say thank you? You might be hardier than a human, but a broken neck is still a broken neck." Wolf doesn't release me. He buries his nose in my neck and inhales deeply. "Gods, you smell good. Or rather, your blood smells good. How you managed to survive this long while walking around like the best kind of candy is beyond me." His lips brush my throat. "Someone should have sucked you dry by now."

I swallow hard, the movement pressing my throat more firmly against his fangs. "Wolf."

"I like the way you say my name, love." He doesn't move back, but he also doesn't close that last minuscule distance between us to draw blood. "Makes me think I'll like it even more if you say it while I'm inside you."

I shiver. "You seemed busy."

"I am. Malachi and I just hit pause for a brief moment." He gentles his grip on my upper arm and then his thumbs brush the sides of my breasts. "It'd be a shame if you got the wrong idea. That look back there was an invitation." He eases me back more firmly against his chest. His cock presses against my ass, which is right around the moment when I realize he's still naked. "Join us."

Join us.

Climb into bed with those superior predators and hope I live long enough to enjoy the consummation. I lick my lips. The unforgivable dark part of me wants to do exactly that. I don't think I like Wolf, and I'm not sure I trust Malachi, but my body doesn't care. It craves pleasure in a way that scares me. One hit might be enough to chain me to them forever. I can't risk it. I refuse to. "No."

"Mmm." He keeps stroking my arms, a relatively innocent touch if I could ignore the naked body and giant cock pressing against my back. "Malachi's made his wishes clear. Your precariously short life is safe with me." His lips brush my throat with each word. "Life. Body. Pleasure."

The man weaves a spell with his words, and it's like my pulse responds to him, each beat of my heart a surge of desire I don't want to feel. If I didn't know better...

I jerk away, and he releases me easily. The feeling doesn't get better with a few feet of distance between us. It's as if he's stroking my body without touching me, sending heat to my breasts and pussy. I press my hand to my chest, realization dawning. "Blood."

"Hmm?"

I stare. "Your bloodline's power is actually *blood*." I suspected as much, but this confirmation staggers me. He could kill me *so easily*, all without raising a finger. A thought and he could send all the blood in my body surging free, draining me in seconds. I shudder. "Stop it."

"If you insist." He shrugs. "I hear it's quite pleasurable."

It is. That's not the problem, though. I am outclassed and outmatched and every second I spend in this house only reconfirms the truth that I'll never have the upper hand. Malachi's fire is scary enough. How can I battle against the very blood in my body? "Don't do that again."

"Fine." Another of those put-upon sighs, but then he grins, his pale eyes lighting up. "I promise not to do it again...until we fuck."

"Who says we're fucking?"

He smooths a hand over his short mohawk, his grin widening. "Fun little side effect of my powers is I can sense blood. Do you know what gets the blood flowing, love?" He doesn't wait for me to answer. "*Desire.*"

Impossible to argue when he already has evidence of it. Especially because I can't blame a bite for it this time. No, it's just my fucked-up head that looks at two men who can easily rip me limb from limb and decides *that* is what'll get me off. "Feeling desire and acting on it are two very different things."

"So they are." Another shrug as if he couldn't give a fuck.

Somehow, in the midst of all this, I forgot he's naked. Now that the shock of his powers has faded a little, it's impossible for me to keep my attention on his face. His skin is several shades lighter than Malachi's, a pale that almost looks unreal. Though he's built leaner than Malachi, too, there's plenty of muscle definition drawing my eye down, down, down, to where his hard cock juts forth.

Fuck.

"Another perk." His amusement is cutting. "With a little blood in my body, I can keep it up for days if I want to. Think of all the pleasure I can give you, love. Come back to the bedroom with us."

I shake my head slowly. The thought of fucking for *days* blows my mind. I can't... I shouldn't... I swallow hard. "I said no."

"So you did." He turns and starts ambling toward Malachi's bedroom. "Ah well, consider this an invitation to watch, then. I promise to be on my best behavior."

"Do you have a best behavior?"

He laughs. "Not even a little bit." Wolf pauses in the doorway. "But Malachi does. He's got enough for all of us." He disappears into the room before I can form a response.

What is there to say?

Walking into that room is a mistake. It's a *choice*. I can't pretend someone forced my hand or I was influenced by anything but my own lust. If I cross that threshold, there's no uncrossing it.

Isn't that what I came here for tonight, though? I didn't bargain on Wolf, but I should have. Malachi as much as told me he and Wolf have a long and complicated history. I might not have fully comprehended they were a package deal. But that doesn't change the fact that apparently they *are*. Can I live with that?

I don't know. There's so much I don't know.

Except...

All I'm doing is stalling, putting off the inevitable. I made my choice already. It might be the first fucking choice I've *ever* made, but it's mine. I close my eyes and inhale slowly. I don't think I'm ready to jump into bed with both of them. But the idea of watching?

I want that. I didn't realize how much I wanted it until Wolf offered that option. A way to dip my toes into the water. I know I'm making excuses to do what I want, but it doesn't matter as I retrace the path to Malachi's door.

The men have their heads close together and are speaking in low voices. They turn as one and I have to fight the instinctive urge to flee. I swallow hard. "I'd like to...watch. If that's okay with both of you."

Wolf grins. "You know it's more than okay with me, love."

I glare at him, but it feels half-hearted. Against my better judgment, I'm starting to like his irreverent attitude. Kind of. I don't know what it says about me, but I'm nowhere close to a place where I want to analyze that. I lick my lips and focus on Malachi. "Is that okay?"

He searches my face for a long moment but must find whatever he's looking for because he nods slowly. "Yes, it's okay."

10

I DON'T KNOW WHAT I EXPECT, BUT IT'S NOT FOR THE vampires to start making out as if I'm not in the room. I look around and finally move to the chair near the bed and sink onto it. Wolf digs his fingers into Malachi's hair and wrenches his head back, deepening the kiss. They're like two titans clashing, powerful predators at the top of their game and grappling for dominance.

It's really, really sexy.

They seem totally lost in each other, which allows me to settle into the strangeness of this situation. To begin to enjoy myself. Malachi shifts in one of those blurring moments and bears Wolf to the bed hard enough to make the other man grunt. The sound reaches across the distance and sends a bolt of pure pleasure through me.

I shift in the chair, pressing my thighs together. It doesn't alleviate the pressure at all. If anything, it makes it worse. Gods, I need to get control of myself.

Except...

Do I?

Malachi brackets Wolf's neck with a big hand, forcing his head to turn to face me. "Look what you've done." He hardly sounds like himself, his voice deeper and containing a rumble that nearly makes *me* moan. "Started something neither of us can finish tonight."

Wolf grins, completely unrepentant. "Speak for yourself. Not all of us have that inconvenient noble streak of yours."

He growls. Literally *growls.* "Mina, stroke your clit or I'm going to come over there and do it for you."

I jolt. "What?"

"You heard me."

I am seriously tempted to call his bluff, but I'm not sure it *is* a bluff. I'm also not sure I want to pull the tiger by his tail. Malachi's managed to restrain himself until now, but if I keep poking him, he might finally force me to put my money where my mouth is.

I reach down beneath the hem of the oversized shirt I'm wearing and touch myself lightly. My breath hisses out before I can stop myself. The evidence of my need wets my fingertips and it's a wonder I haven't soaked through the chair. I lean back against it and drag my middle finger over my clit. This time, I can't stop my moan.

Both men give moans of their own, the merging sounds making me look up and freeze. They're both staring at my hand, their eyes gone molten with their respective magics. Malachi drags his thumb along Wolf's jaw. "Pull your shirt up, little dhampir. Show us."

We're dancing on a bladed tightrope. One wrong step and this will blow up right in our faces. Or maybe only mine. How far can I push these two before I end up in bed and we all throw my hesitance right out the window? Do I *want* that?

I pull up my shirt before I can admit the answer to that question, baring myself from the waist down. After the slightest hesitation, I spread my legs a little, angling so they can see everything. Wolf starts to sit up, but Malachi pins him down and reaches between them with one hand. I can't see exactly what he's doing, but a few seconds later, Wolf tenses and moans. Malachi begins moving and... Oh. *Oh.* He's fucking Wolf.

Oh my gods.

I stroke myself faster, watching the roll of his hips, watching the way Wolf's muscles flex as he tries to take Malachi's cock deeper. Wolf curses softly. "He's got a giant cock, love. Feels so fucking good inside me." He grins, his eyes going crimson. "Just imagine how good he's going to feel inside you."

I don't know if I *can* imagine it, but my mind is only too happy to make a liar out of me. Desire spikes and I have to force myself to slow down, to draw this out. I don't want to come too fast. "I'm imagining it," I whisper.

Malachi slows down, seeming to give me his full attention despite being seated deeply in Wolf's ass. "We aren't fucking you."

"Pity," Wolf murmurs.

"We aren't fucking you," Malachi repeats more firmly. A slow smile pulls at the edges of his lips, an expression downright wicked. "But you're welcome to Wolf's mouth while I fuck *him*."

That's a mistake.

I ignore the voice and nod. "Yes, I want that."

"Thought you might." He pulls out of Wolf and takes the other man's jaw in a tight grip, forcing him to meet Malachi's eyes. "One wrong move and I gut you."

Wolf laughs. "It's always gutting with you. That shit *hurts*, Malachi."

"Which is why it's a deterrent and a punishment." He leans back and slaps Wolf's side. "On the floor in front of her."

He moves slowly, obeying but doing it on his own timeline. Wolf kneels in front of my chair. He looks at me for a moment and then moves in a rush, grabbing my shirt and hauling it over my head. I'm naked in an instant and he bands his arm over my lower stomach as I lurch forward, instinctively grabbing for the shirt. "Ah ah. Give our Malachi something to look at." Another of those infectious grins. "He's a breast man and yours are superior."

I'm still trying to form a response as he lowers himself and takes my pussy with his mouth. There's no other way to describe it. Wolf doesn't ease into it. He doesn't taste. He simply devours me. I moan, every muscle going molten even as every nerve ending lights up.

Malachi moves to kneel at Wolf's back. I catch sight of a bottle of lube in his hand and then he's fucking Wolf. It must feel amazing, because the other man moans and starts fucking me with his tongue.

I don't know where to look, what to feel. Wolf's hands gripping my thighs, his eyes crimson as he edges me closer and closer to orgasm. At the lean strength of his body, which flexes with each thrust Malachi makes.

Or at Malachi himself.

He has one hand on Wolf's hip and the other on the opposite shoulder, holding the other man in place as he fucks him in short, brutal strokes. But his eyes are on me. His gaze touches on my mouth, my neck, my breasts, before moving down my stomach to where Wolf's head is buried between my thighs.

"She tastes divine, doesn't she? Just as sweet there as she is in her veins."

Wolf makes a sound of agreement but doesn't lift his head. He works my clit with his tongue, finding the touch that has me clenching in response and repeating it mercilessly. I reach back over my head to grip the chair. The position puts my body on display, and the way fire flickers in Malachi's eyes speaks to how much he likes the sight.

Words rise up, words I'm not sure I won't regret.

I changed my mind. Fuck me. Fuck me until we forget all the reasons this might be a mistake.

My orgasm hits me before they can slip free, barreling into me and bowing my back. I cry out as the pleasure goes on and on and on. Malachi finally curses and grabs the back of Wolf's neck, wrenching him off me. Or trying to. The other man drags me with him, taking me half out of the chair. I let loose a startled cry, but then it's too late. I'm on the floor with them.

Malachi curses and Wolf pins me beneath him.

I freeze at the feeling of his cock pressed against me, at his face so fucking close. His beauty is downright otherworldly, and I know I should be scared, but I can't quite manage it. I lick my lips, and he follows the movement. One thrust and he'll be inside me. I can feel Malachi holding his hips, holding him back from that last little bit of distance.

"I'll hold still, love." His voice is pure sin, as tempting as Lucifer himself. "Rub yourself all over me while Malachi fucks my ass."

Reckless doesn't begin to cover agreeing to this, but I'm already nodding. My body doesn't care about the risks. His hard length pressing against my pussy is a temptation I can't resist. "Yes."

Malachi grips Wolf's throat and bends him back a little, shifting so his face is nearly kissably close to me. He looks at me, but his words are all for Wolf. "That virgin pussy is mine, Wolf. If you fuck her tonight, I'll rip your goddamn throat out."

Something like shock flares on Wolf's face, but it's gone in an instant, replaced by what I'm coming to recognize as his default expression: a mocking smile. "And here I thought we were sharing the pretty toy."

"We will." Malachi says it so casually, as if it's a foregone conclusion. I'm not sure he's wrong. "But not the first time."

I swallow hard. "Do I get a say in this?"

His expression goes downright forbidding. "Not tonight, you don't."

I start to argue, but what's the point? He's honoring my wishes, even if I'm questioning my own fortitude to maintain those lines. I reach past Wolf to brush my fingers against Malachi's mouth. He holds perfectly still, letting me drag my thumb over his bottom lip. I shift my touch over his jaw. "Okay."

"Not arguing?"

"No, not arguing." I shift a little, all too aware of Wolf's body against mine, of Malachi very carefully not adding his weight into the mix. "Thank you."

He grabs my wrist and turns to press a kiss to my palm. "Now be a good girl and rub your pussy all over Wolf's cock until he comes." He starts moving again, resuming his fucking, each thrust making Wolf jolt against me a little. It's beyond sexy.

I arch up as Wolf bears down, closing the distance so there's no chance of him slipping inside. I roll my hips, rubbing myself up and down his length. It's positively decadent, the sensation heightened by the feeling of playing with fire. One wrong move and we cross the line Malachi drew in the sand. I don't necessarily *want* to cross the line, but the knowledge it's there heightens my pleasure.

Wolf catches my hips, urging me into longer strokes that send my thoughts scattering like flower petals in the wind. "I bet you feel empty right now, don't you? Needy."

He's right, but I can't catch my breath to tell him so. Each stroke has me dancing closer to the edge. "Gods, Wolf."

He goes stock-still. "Fuck, but I like it when you say my name." He kisses my neck. "What do you need, love?"

I answer before I can think about the wisdom of it. "Bite me."

He doesn't hesitate before sinking his fangs into my throat. I grab his hips and frantically chase my orgasm. One stroke. Two.

Then I'm coming, crying out in a ragged breath as I do. Except it doesn't stop. The orgasm rolls over me again and again, and I can't stop writhing, rubbing against him, trying to get closer, desperate for something I can barely conceptualize.

"*Wolf.*" Malachi's snarl slams me back into myself. He's farther away than I expect. I catch sight of him standing in the bathroom doorway, a cloth in his hand.

Wolf and I both go still. My heart is beating so hard, I feel dizzy. Or maybe that's the danger screaming through my veins at the feeling of the broad head of Wolf's cock pressing against my entrance. "Wait."

"She's so wet." I can't see Wolf's expression with his face buried against my neck, but his voice is downright feral. "So tight, Malachi. So needy for a cock." His hips flex, pushing into me the tiniest bit. "Might be worth getting my throat torn out." He strokes a hand down my side, but I can't tell if he's trying to soothe me or hold me down.

Another of those tiny flexes and he pushes farther into me. It feels good and bad and, oh gods, I don't know if I want him to stop.

I don't get a chance to decide. A blur of movement and then something hot and wet hits my chest and stomach. I freeze, my fangs aching at the copper scent filling the air.

Wolf slumps to the side of me, bleeding from his throat. Even as I watch, the wound starts healing, fusing together faster than I could have imagined possible. That doesn't change the fact that Malachi just…ripped out his throat.

And then Malachi is there, covering me with his big body.

Wolf's blood slicks our skin against each other, the scent of it only heightening my desire. I reach down with a shaking hand and drag my fingers through where it coats my breasts.

Malachi catches my wrist as I raise my fingers to my mouth. "Not yet."

"But—"

"I said I wouldn't do this." He curses long and hard, looking like an entirely different person, a creature more beast than man. "Say yes, Mina."

No mistaking what he means. No pretending I don't know what I'm going to get if I agree. I don't know if he'll let me walk out of this room if I tell him no, but I believe with my entire heart he'd try.

I don't want to say no.

I take a shuddering breath, allowing myself to be lost in the flames in his dark eyes. There are so many things I once believed I should want, but there's no place for *should* here. There is no future, no past, nothing but this moment where the two of us perch poised on the precipice of no return. Wolf, too.

I lick my lips, tasting Wolf's blood there, too. It zings through me, just as potent as Malachi's but different. His tastes as hot as his flames do. Wolf's is spicy and somehow barbed. It tastes better than alcohol, but I knew my answer before it hit my veins. "Yes."

11

MALACHI KISSES ME. IT'S JUST AS CONSUMING AS EVERY other time, and I dig my bloody hands into his hair as I lose myself in his taste. I'm only vaguely aware of him moving our bodies, hitching one of my legs up and around his waist. He drags his cock over my pussy and then his broad head is pressed against my entrance.

I tense, but he doesn't shove inside. He leans back enough to meet my gaze. "The first time can be painful."

Trying to think past the buzzing in my veins is almost too difficult. "I know that."

"I'm going to bite you to negate that." He hesitates, suddenly looking more like the man I've been spending so much time with rather than the monster who just ripped his friend's throat out so he could fuck me first. "Are you sure, Mina?"

I pull on his hair, frustration getting the better part of me. "I've never had a choice, Malachi. Not once in my fucking life. I'm saying yes, choosing this. Stop questioning it and fuck me."

Wolf gives a wet laugh from where he's leaning against the side of the bed, his hand against his healing throat. "You heard her."

"I'll deal with *you* presently."

"With more orgasms, I hope."

Malachi gives an exasperated rumble. "Shut up, Wolf."

"Yes, Sir."

I whimper. "Malachi, *please.*"

He hesitates for so long, I think he might have changed his mind. But before I can say anything else, he curses and strikes, sinking his fangs into my throat on the opposite side of where Wolf did. At the same time, he drives into me. I get a blast of pure agony and then the pleasure of the bite takes over, washing it all away in a tidal wave of need. I think I scream. Maybe I black out. I don't know.

The next moment, I come back to myself, my legs locked around Malachi's hips and my fingers tangled in his hair as I rise to meet each slow thrust. Pain and pleasure dance together in an elegant symphony. "Oh *fuck.*"

Malachi slows down and lifts his head a little. "Stay with me."

I run my hands down his broad back and dig my nails into his ass. "Don't stop." I moan. "Don't you dare stop."

His pace hitches, but he recovers quickly, kissing me as he resumes that slow fucking. He's big, and he feels bigger inside me than he did when he was pressed against me. I revel in the fullness, in the way my body stretches to accommodate him.

"Malachi."

We go still at the warning in Wolf's tone. Malachi shudders out a breath. "I have it under control."

"Do you? Because I have no desire to die in a fire because you're so lost in our Mina's sweet pussy that you burn the house down around us."

"I have it under control," Malachi repeats.

It's right around then I notice the flames behind him are roaring high enough it looks like they might burst out of the fireplace at any moment. I should care, but I really don't. I dig my fingers into his ass again. "Don't. Stop."

"I won't, little dhampir. I won't ever stop." He kisses me again and resumes moving, driving me higher and higher.

Part of me wishes I could blame this on the bite, but it's pure Malachi. He's overwhelming, and the fact that we're fucking while covered in Wolf's blood only makes this more depraved, more perfect.

I catch sight of the pulse thrumming in his neck and bite him without thinking. It's messy—my fangs really *are* too small to serve their purpose—but Malachi shoves his arms between my body and the floor, lifting me closer to him so I have better access to his neck. So he has better access to my pussy. He shifts the angle just enough that, combined with his blood coating my tongue, I scream my way through another orgasm.

It's like lighting a match in a room full of gunpowder. He crushes me to him and then he's driving into me just shy of brutally, rumbling my name as he comes.

We slump to the floor and I stare at the ceiling, wondering

if the stars themselves have been rearranged. It feels like they should be. The world is no longer the same as it was an hour ago.

Nothing will ever be the same again.

"Malachi." Wolf's tone is dry. "Control yourself."

I twist just enough to see the fire has escaped the hearth and is snaking its way toward us. Malachi curses and it immediately reverses course, shooting into the fireplace and returning to a normal-sized flame. He eases off me. "Did I hurt you?"

"Not in any permanent way." I ache all over, but it's nothing compared to the pleasure pulsing in time with my heartbeat. I lift a hand to my mouth. I feel...different. Strange. I give myself a shake. Of course I feel different. I just had sex for the first time. More, I just all but agreed to have sex with *both* these vampires in the near future. I am a stranger to the woman I was two weeks ago.

Malachi sits up and leans over to peel Wolf's hand off his throat. The skin there is new and pink but intact. "Sorry."

"No, you're not."

"No, I'm not." He grabs Wolf's chin and pulls him forward into a quick kiss. "Maybe one day you'll be able to resist pushing."

"Unlikely. If it hasn't happened yet, it's not going to."

The fact that they're joking after Malachi ripped out Wolf's throat is so purely *vampire*, I almost laugh. But the events of the last hour are catching up to me quickly and I'm starting to shake. Malachi notices first. He stands, scooping me into his arms. "On your feet, Wolf."

"So bossy." Wolf staggers up and follows us into the bathroom. Malachi's bathroom is even bigger than mine, with a tub large enough to be termed a pool. Wolf moves to turn the tap on without prompting, but Malachi heads directly for the shower. I understand the moment he sets me on my feet and I get a good look at the three of us. I knew we were covered in blood, of course, but seeing it now that the adrenaline and lust are fading hits differently. We look like we've just survived a massacre.

I let Malachi tow me beneath the spray, but then I try to pull my hand from his. "I can wash myself."

"Hush."

I blink. "You did not just *hush* me."

"He did." Wolf steps into the space behind me, and suddenly the roomy shower feels almost crowded. He catches my hips. "Malachi is feeling guilty. Let him make it up to you."

I look up at the vampire in question and I'm shocked to find that Wolf's right. There's something akin to remorse in those dark eyes. He and Wolf guide me farther into the water and the blood runs off my skin in waves. I'm so busy trying to process the guilt, I let them wash me.

It feels...good. For once, it's not sexual, but the sensation of skin against skin is almost too much for me. I've been touched more tonight than I have in the past five years combined. Gods, that's depressing, but after I turned eighteen, touching meant a beating or some other kind of torment. Better to avoid it altogether. I didn't realize how much I missed it until now.

Once they're satisfied, Malachi shuts off the water and they guide me to the tub, now filled with steaming water. It stings as I step into it, but the heat quickly soaks into my bones and I sink down with a groan.

I don't know why I'm surprised the men follow. They take up positions across from me, creating a little triangle with the three of us. The tub is so large, there's still plenty of room, which might make me laugh if I had the energy for it. As it is, I'm suddenly so exhausted, I can barely keep my head above water.

Malachi sighs. "Come here, Mina." He doesn't wait for me to respond, just reaches over, grabs my wrist, and tows me over to half float in his lap. He guides my head to his shoulder, and the position allows me to relax fully. He carefully sets his hands on my hips, keeping me anchored in place. "I didn't mean for it to happen like this."

"There he is." Wolf laughs. "So eager for that guilt. She said yes. That's consent."

"I promised I wouldn't."

I give in to the feeling of gravity weighing my eyelids down. "I wouldn't have come to your room if I didn't want to end up in some variation of what happened." It's the truth, even if I couldn't admit it to myself until the moment Wolf tempted me with something I hadn't realized I wanted. Worrying about doing this the *right way* is silly. There is no right way when you live in a world of vampires and blood wards and sacrifices. Which reminds me... "Is there another way to break a blood ward beyond killing someone?"

Both men go still and I open my eyes to find them exchanging a look. Wolf finally shrugs. "There's a theory other supernatural creatures might have ways to do it, but I've never seen it first-hand. You'd have to fill the space with so much power the ward couldn't contain it, but without a sacrifice, it's impossible for a vampire to do it."

That's what I'm afraid of.

It's not that I think Malachi will kill me. Foolish or no, I trust he means me no harm. But as long as that blood ward is up, we're both trapped here. Now that we've crossed the line of no return, it's theoretically only a matter of time before I get pregnant and my father comes to collect me. No matter how powerful Malachi is, he's no match for my father and his turned minions. They have numbers on their side, and my father is also a bloodline vampire. Malachi won't win, which means I'll be carted back to the colony until I give birth and they decide they no longer need me.

There has to be another solution. There *has* to be.

"Don't worry about that, Mina." Malachi's chest rumbles at my back as he speaks. "You're safe here."

Safe.

What a foreign concept. I'm not safe here. None of us are. Not while we stay where my father can reach us.

I close my eyes again and relax back against him. "We'll find another way out."

"We, huh?" Wolf's tone is lightly mocking. "She gets one cock inside her and we're all a big happy family."

"You're free to go whenever you want, Wolf." Malachi rests his chin on top of my head. "Nothing's keeping you here."

A pause, and I have a feeling they're doing one of those silent exchanges. I don't open my eyes. No matter what I was feeling in the moment, I'm honestly *not* sure of Wolf. I won't ask him to stay, especially since he's not trapped here like we are.

Finally, Wolf gives a dramatic sigh. "I suppose I'll stick around for a bit." A calculated pause. "Rylan mentioned he might meet me here at some point, but you know how he is."

Malachi tenses beneath me. "You're just *now* telling me?"

"It slipped my mind."

"I'm sure it did." Malachi curses. "Convenient, that."

"Isn't it?"

I finally drag my eyes open. "Who's Rylan?"

"Another bloodline."

That shocks some of the exhaustion from my system. "*Another* bloodline? I thought most of you were scattered or loners?" Three of the bloodlines, including my father's, are still in power in their respective territories, even if their numbers are low. But I was under the impression the remaining four were scattered to the winds.

"We are." Wolf's got that strange smile on his face, as if he's telling an inside joke. "But the vampire community isn't so large that any of us are strangers, especially those of us who have been around for a few centuries."

There's more there, more he isn't saying, but I don't have the energy to drag it out of him tonight. I twist a little to look at Malachi. "Is Rylan a problem?"

He hesitates, clearly torn. "No," he finally says. "We have a complicated history, but he's not an enemy."

"So confident," Wolf murmurs. "I wonder if Rylan feels the same way. Especially now you have this delicious little dhampir riding your cock."

"Fuck off, Wolf."

"Tempting."

I look at them both. "Another ex?"

Their silence confirms my guess hit right on the mark. I barely resist the urge to sink beneath the surface of the water and scream. It's not exactly surprising Malachi has people who care about him, complicated history or no, but I don't look forward to another conversation about sacrificing me to get his freedom. And yes, maybe there's a little jealousy there for these two vampires that have known him long enough to *have* a complicated history.

I rise on shaking legs but brush off Malachi's hand raised in an offer to help. "I'm very tired."

"Mina—"

Wolf moves, blurring out of the tub. I barely get a chance to tense before he wraps me up in a large towel. He grins down at me, obviously enjoying the minor chaos he's stirred up. "What our darling Malachi won't say is that he wants you to stay."

"He's more than capable of speaking for himself." I slant a glance in his direction. "Or ripping out throats when words don't work."

Wolf gives a deep, happy laugh. "I like you, Mina. Most mortals would be rocking in a corner after all that bloody fucking. You're interesting."

"I'm pretty sure you're certifiably insane."

"Guilty." He grins and shrugs. "You learn to enjoy the ride."

Against my better judgment, I find my lips curving. "I'll keep that in mind."

"Do." He squeezes my shoulders, hands curiously gentle on me despite his irreverence. "Stay, love. We'll be on our best behavior."

"I don't believe that for a second."

"Guilty again."

I hear Malachi rising out of the tub and the water draining, but I don't look over. My instincts are to retreat and lick my proverbial wounds until the ground feels steadier beneath my feet. But I can't deny the thought of letting these two ground me is attractive. Maybe it's weak, but I can't really bring myself to care. "Okay. I'll stay."

12

I WAKE UP BETWEEN TWO MALE BODIES. I KEEP MY EYES closed and fight not to tense, waiting for my brain to catch up with my circumstances. As sleep fades away completely, the events of the last twenty-four hours comes back to me.

Gods, things keep happening too fast. It feels like the entire world has changed its shape around me. It's so incredibly tempting to pull the covers over my head and hide away to avoid thinking about it, but I haven't survived this long by ignoring the reality of my circumstances. It's better to deal with the hard truths up front than to ignore them until they're literally ripping your throat out.

Wolf's back is pressed against mine, and when I open my eyes, I find Malachi watching me. I lift a brow. "Creepy of you."

"You were thinking hard over there." He presses a finger to the spot between my brows. "Regrets?"

"No, nothing like that." It's even true. I don't make a habit of regretting my choices, but this goes beyond that. My feelings for Malachi are a pulse in my blood I can't ignore. It's more than desire, more than lust, even more complicated than something as ridiculous as love. I don't understand it, but I don't have to fully understand it in order to acknowledge its existence.

I worry my bottom lip. "How are we going to get out of this?" Will there even be a *we* after we do? Or will he grab his freedom with both hands and ride off into the sunset, happy to no longer be chained to a cranky dhampir with rage issues. "And after—"

Malachi twines a strand of my hair around his fingers. "When you've lived as long as I have, you learn to recognize the important things."

"Like freedom."

He snorts. "Like *you*, Mina. I've never met anyone quite like you."

"You mean you've never tasted anyone quite like me." I don't know why I'm being so stubborn about this, but what he's saying is impossible. We've known each other a little over a week at this point. There's no way he's feeling some kind of mystical connection to me. It's far more likely he finds me valuable in a different way. That's how vampires work, after all. Power and ambition above the softer emotions. Always.

"I mean what I said." He tugs lightly on my hair. "But I respect it'll take you longer to trust me, given your history."

"That is remarkably patronizing of you."

He chuckles. "I'm trying to tell you I like you."

Like feels too tame a word to use for what flares between Malachi and me. I'm not sure what to say to that, so I swallow hard and change the subject. "So how do we get out of this mess?"

"If Wolf is to be believed—"

"I am." Behind me, Wolf turns around and slings an arm over my hip. He doesn't *quite* press his hard cock to my ass, but I can feel the tension of it behind me.

Malachi snorts. "Then Rylan will be here shortly. Between the three of us, we can figure out a solution." He shoots a sharp glance over my shoulder. "A solution that *doesn't* involve your death, Mina."

"Tsk, tsk, after last night, I'm not particularly fond of the idea of our Mina bleeding out for your freedom. Why waste all that *delicious* blood on something as mundane as freedom?" Wolf's breath ghosts the back of my neck. "We'll find another way."

"As simple as that."

"As horrendously complicated as that." Wolf sounds like he relishes the challenge, but even after knowing him such a short time, I'm not surprised he's perverse like that.

I relax against him, soaking up all this skin-to-skin contact. It's heady and intoxicating, nearly as much as the sex was last night. I can *touch* these men as much as I want. I lightly stroke my hand down Malachi's impressive chest. "I suppose we'll have to keep ourselves occupied until then."

His muscles jump beneath my fingertips. "You need to eat something." He searches my face. "I've also ordered you some iron supplements. Even with the blood exchange, you're paler than you were when arriving here."

Something in my chest warms even as my logical side points out he's just looking after his food source. I'm no good to them if I pass out constantly from being anemic. That's the most likely reason Malachi is acting like a mother hen. Despite my reasonable explanation, the feeling in my chest gets warmer. I find myself smiling. "I'm not quite ready to get out of bed yet."

Behind me, Wolf blurs. One moment I'm on my side, facing Malachi, and the next Wolf is on top of me, settling between my thighs. He grins down at me, flashing fang. "No point in worrying about anything until Rylan appears. There are better ways to occupy our time."

It's against my nature to push worry aside when I can poke and prod at a situation until I find a way forward. But it's hard to remember with Malachi's brooding presence next to me and Wolf's warmth pressing me into the mattress. I stare up at him, tracing the carved lines of his cheekbones and those eerie colorless eyes. He's beautiful. I registered it before, but there's something about the softness of sleep still lingering in his expression that pushes him from being terrifying to just being breathtaking.

I reach up with a cautious hand and stroke my thumb along his cheekbone. "You're very, very pretty."

"I know." His grin widens. "I'm going to kiss you now."

It's not quite a question, but I want to kiss him. I don't know what it says about me that I had Malachi last night—have him right next to me right now—and all I can think about is kissing Wolf again. But then, Malachi seems just as into this as I am.

They're right; there's nothing to be done right now. Or maybe that's the excuse I cling to as I nod slowly. "Okay."

He starts to lean down and pauses to glance at Malachi, who's watching us with a small smile on his lips. Wolf gives his hand a pointed look. "Are *you* going to behave?"

"Do you want me to?"

Wolf laughs. "As enjoyable as it was to watch you fuck her while covered in my blood, I'd like to feel Mina coming on my cock more than I want a repeat right now." He settles more firmly between my thighs and thrusts a little. "Sore?"

"No." In fact, I feel better than I have since the first time I took Malachi's blood. Energized and downright glowy. I'm sure if I had access to a mirror, I'd find I look a mess, but it doesn't matter right now. I'm not sure what it says about me that I desperately want to fuck Wolf just as much as I wanted—still want—Malachi, but I'm past questioning these things. Everyone is obviously into this and it's not like vampire culture is overly monogamous. That whole mates-for-life thing is nice in theory, but when your life spans centuries, even the most intense love can shift and change. I've noticed partner hopping just from watching the way the vampires in my father's colony operate. There's no reason to think this is abnormal.

Again, I feel like I'm grasping for a reason to do this. It only means what I let it mean.

My life has been so devoid of pleasure up to this point. Is it any surprise I'm desperate to grab on to any bit of it I can touch, to glut myself on it with these two devastatingly gorgeous men? Maybe I'll wake up in a day or two and wonder what the hell I'm doing, but I don't care right now. I just want to feel good.

And yet...

I press a hand to Wolf's chest. For all his pushiness, he goes still immediately. I glance at Malachi. "Are you okay with this?"

He raises his brows. "Why wouldn't I be?"

"Um." When he says it like that, I feel silly for even asking. "Because we had sex last night?"

"And I fucked Wolf last night."

Right. I'd almost forgotten about that particular detail. I worry my bottom lip. "Still."

Malachi props his head on one hand and looks down at me. "Stop worrying about what you *should* want and focus on what you *do* want."

"Like it's that easy."

"It's exactly that easy." He sifts his fingers through my hair and then over Wolf's arm. "When you're immortal, the reasons for not taking what you want don't hold up."

The reminder that they'll live on forever while I age and eventually die is almost enough to dispel the lust Wolf is weaving around me. I could swear he hasn't moved, but he's got my leg hitched up around his waist and his cock is pressing against me in a way that feels so good, I can barely stand it. I lick my lips. "I'm not immortal."

"Not yet." Malachi kisses me before I can ask him what the hell he's talking about. Humans and dhampirs can be turned, but I'm an anomaly. A dhampir with no power of my own. I might be an anomaly when it comes to the other rules, too.

I could break the kiss, could argue, could demand more information, but I am so goddamn tired of running around like a hamster on a wheel. No matter how hard I fight, how many scenarios I run, I am still trapped. My fate is still in the hands of other people.

I really am a coward, because I push away those thoughts and grab the pleasure the two of them are offering me with both hands. Malachi moves back and then Wolf's there, nipping my bottom lip. He tastes just as spicy as he smells, something that defies explanation. The why doesn't matter, though. It's enough that it simply is.

He reaches between us with his free hand and begins dragging his cock through my folds. Up and down, spreading my wetness around, teasing me even as he kisses every thought out of my head. Just when I'm about to pull back to beg him to just fuck me, he notches his cock at my entrance.

And then he's inside me.

I was too distracted by Malachi's bite to fully appreciate that first stroke last night, but being filled by Wolf is an experience I don't have words for. He's big, but he feels different from Malachi. I exhale in a rush as his hips meet mine, sealing us together.

"Fuck, she feels good, Malachi."

"I know." His voice has gone deep, gained a little of that sexy growl that I'm starting to crave. He's still got my hand in his and he laces our fingers together as his friend starts to fuck me in slow, rolling strokes. The feeling makes me go soft and molten, each thrust rubbing against something inside me that has the top of my head in danger of spinning off.

Wolf moves back, bracing his hands on either side of my ribs, and looks down our bodies. I follow his gaze, and *fuck*. The sight of his cock sliding in and out of me, of his body rolling with each thrust, of the way I spread to take him deeper... "*Wolf*." I moan.

He shortens his strokes, rubbing that spot over and over again. "Malachi."

I blink up at him, a part of me wondering why he's saying Malachi's name while he's inside me, but then Malachi shifts closer and snakes a hand down my stomach to stroke my clit. Did I think the sight of Wolf fucking me was enough to send me to the moon? Malachi's fingers lightly rubbing my clit in the way I love, Wolf's cock inside me hitting that spot... Gods, it's too much.

I dig my heels into the mattress as I orgasm, but they hold me in place. And they don't stop. The pleasure just keeps rolling over me again and again, until Wolf's strokes hitch and he drives into me with a rough curse. I swear I can feel him coming, filling me up, but I don't get a chance to wonder if it's my imagination because Malachi gives his shoulder a light shove and Wolf flops onto his back next to me.

Before I can mourn the loss of him, Malachi drags me over and turns me so my back is to his chest. He hitches one of my legs over his hip and then his cock is wedging its way inside me. He's broader than Wolf, and even though we were just fucking, he has to work to sink all the way into me.

"*Fuck.*" I reach out to claw at the sheets, but Wolf is there, catching my hands and moving to nuzzle at my breasts. He palms them as Malachi grips my thigh with one big hand and spreads me farther, sinking deeper yet.

"Don't bite her."

"Spoilsport," Wolf murmurs against my nipple. He works his way down my stomach, trailing lightly teasing kisses. I tense as I realize where he's going, but neither I nor Malachi stop him as he settles at my hips and leans forward to lick my clit.

I arch back against Malachi and then moan. This feels dirty and decadent and I can't quite believe it's happening.

Malachi begins to fuck me. It's nothing like last night. Not brutal at all. It's almost…lazy. As if he plans to memorize every inch of me. Wolf's licking me in the same way. It's as if they have time now they got the first orgasm out of the way. As if they want to enjoy this as much as I'm enjoying it.

I can't afford to think too closely about that. I'm not capable of it right now anyway. All I can do is take what they give me.

Then Wolf's mouth is gone and Malachi jolts behind me. I lean forward enough to see the other man biting his thigh, mirth lighting his crimson eyes. Malachi curses and then he's driving into me in rough thrusts. "You fucking bastard."

Wolf gives one last pull from his thigh and then his mouth is back at my pussy. This time, he isn't messing around. He sucks on my clit as Malachi pounds into me hard enough that they have to hold me in place between them to keep us from inching across the mattress.

And then I'm coming and nothing else matters. Malachi thrusts again and again and then yanks me back onto his cock as he grinds into me. We exhale as one, but he makes no move to pull out of me. Wolf kisses my lower stomach and then moves up to flop down beside us. "That was a fun appetizer."

I blink at him. "Appetizer."

"Yes." He turns onto his side and props his head in his hand. "I haven't fucked Malachi in years, and you're a delightful new snack." He leans forward, his eyes still crimson with lust. "I said I can go for days, love, and I meant it."

Malachi curses and plants a hand in the center of Wolf's face, shoving him back. "She's half human. She needs to eat."

"Pity." Wolf throws his arm over his eyes. "Fine. Go do your human things."

"Wolf." Malachi grips my hip, keeping me from moving. "Go put something together for breakfast."

Wolf lifts his arm enough to give us a long-suffering look. "If you insist, but I'm getting my cock sucked when I come back."

"Go."

He huffs and rolls off the bed. Even though I don't know him well, I can still tell he's putting on a show as he walks out of the room, well aware we're watching him walk away.

The door barely shuts behind him when Malachi strokes his hands up my body to cup my breasts. "Tired?"

As if I can't feel him getting hard inside me again. I shiver. "Don't stop."

13

"MINA."

Gods, the way this vampire says my name. I start to twist to try to see him, but he blurs, pulling out of me just long enough to push me onto my back and then easing his cock into me again. His eyes are pure black. Malachi thrusts a little, his gaze going to my mouth when I moan. "Mina," he says again.

I don't know what he's going to say. I'm just not ready for this to be over. At some point, we're going to have to talk about plans and blood wards and my father, but not yet.

I dig my hands into his hair and arch up to kiss his jaw. "Don't stop."

Malachi growls and then we're moving again. This time, he keeps us sealed together as he rolls onto his back and takes me with him, leaving me straddling him, his cock still seated deep inside me. "Ride me."

The new position makes me feel almost exposed. He's still got a grip on me, but it's light as I roll my hips, moving slowly until I find a rhythm that feels good. Fuck, what am I talking about? Everything feels good.

Having Malachi beneath me, seeing his powerful body spread out as if for my pleasure… It's intoxicating in the extreme. We don't need to speak at all. Not when my body already knows what to do, not when he's filling me so perfectly. I plant my hands on his chest and begin chasing my own pleasure.

I'm almost there, so close to coming, when an unfamiliar dry voice cuts through my pleasure. "So *this* is why you haven't bothered to find a way out of this cage."

I freeze for half a second and then scramble off Malachi. He lets me, sitting up to shield me with his big body. Has he gotten bigger in the last couple days? I hadn't really noticed, but now I'm sure of it. I look over his shoulder at the man standing in the doorway. He's a white guy with a close-cropped beard and short dark hair, and he's wearing an honest-to-god suit.

Malachi tenses. "Rylan."

Rylan, the one Wolf said would show up at some point. He couldn't be more different from the wild blond vampire. He looks like some kind of CEO, and I swear the room dropped ten degrees when he entered. I shiver, and he flicks a look at me. His blue eyes go even colder. "Leave while the grown-ups talk, little girl."

My shiver turns into a full-out shudder and goose bumps rise across my skin in a wave of warning. Even without knowing he's a bloodline vampire beforehand, the sheer power in his eyes would tell me an apex predator has entered the room. I start to inch toward the other side of the bed, but Malachi reaches out and grabs my hand. "Stay."

Rylan raises his brows. "Keep your pet if you insist, but you know she's a trap in a pretty package. You were about to come inside her." His upper lip curls. "Idiot."

"Make sure to tell Wolf how you really feel because he filled her up not thirty minutes ago."

The crass words make me flinch. I'd forgotten. Gods, how could I have forgotten? Rylan scares me, but he's not wrong. Imagine my father's delight if he manages to trap Wolf with a child. He might love that even more than Malachi since Malachi is chained to this property by the blood ward, and that kind of cage could never hold Wolf.

I yank my hand out of Malachi's, and this time he lets me, but he starts to turn in my direction. "Mina—"

"This pretty trap is taking herself elsewhere." It's too late. Far too late. Unless it isn't? I snag my oversized shirt off the floor and yank it over my head. I have to catch Wolf before he gets back to this room. *He* can leave without an issue, can get me what I need to make sure this isn't a mistake of epic proportions.

I stop a few feet away from the door Rylan still hasn't shifted away from. "Move."

He stares me down. "I should kill you now and solve all our problems. Can't breed if you're dead."

The fire has nearly died down to ashes, but it flares high as Malachi climbs to his feet, eerily slow. "Watch your words or, friend or not, you'll lose your head."

Rylan's eyes widen just a fraction. "You fool."

"Fool or not, it stands."

He shakes his head and finally moves back. Even knowing those couple of feet won't make much difference if he decided to make a grab for me, I inch out the door and take off running for the kitchen. I find Wolf staring at a pot of water suspiciously. It's odd enough that it almost distracts me. "What are you doing?"

"How long does water take to boil? I mean, honestly, this is just plebeian." He glances at me and narrows his eyes. "You're scared. What happened?"

"Rylan is here." I jump forward when he starts to blur toward the door, barely getting there before him. "Wait!"

Wolf stops short. "He and Malachi need a referee or they're going to rip this house down to the foundation."

Even with that risk, this is too large to ignore. Especially when every hour counts and we're quite a ways from the nearest human town. "Wolf, wait."

He narrows his eyes. "What's going on?"

I don't know how I'm supposed to handle this, so I just blurt it out. "You came inside me." When he starts to smirk, I rush on. "If I get pregnant with your baby, my father will use it to collar you. I can't let that happen. Not to you or Malachi." I lift my hands but let them drop before I touch him. "The humans have something called the morning-after pill. Or Plan B. Or something like that. I need you to get it for me. The sooner, the better."

He searches my expression, looking uncharacteristically serious. "You'd go to such lengths?"

"It's a pill. It's not like I'm agreeing to surgery with no anesthetic." When he keeps staring, I wrap my arms around myself.

"Look, I know why I was sent here, and I know there's no happy ending for this for me, but at least I can make sure I don't screw you guys over. Malachi can't go. Neither can I. It has to be you."

He reaches out and catches my chin lightly. "You know if you did end up pregnant, I'd simply whisk you away to somewhere your father can never find you."

That's vaguely comforting as a plan of last resort, but that doesn't create a fix for all our problems right now. "What about Malachi?"

"When you have forever, it gives you time to figure out alternative solutions." He shrugs. "Most likely, once I secure you, I'll snatch up some human and haul them back here to break the blood ward and free Malachi."

"Let's just shelve the idea of murder for the time being." I hesitate. "And maybe get condoms, too? If you want to keep fucking?"

His grin is quick and wicked. "Oh, love, we are *definitely* going to keep fucking." He kisses me, and then he's gone, moving so fast my hair lifts in the breeze of his passing.

I exhale slowly. There's nothing to do but wait now. I know I should eat, but my stomach is tied up in knots. I'll just grab something and take it back to my room. Barricading myself in sounds like a good plan right about now. I know it's more emotional comfort than actually a deterrent for a murderous vampire, but it's better than nothing.

I feel the cold as I shut off the burner. It's the only indication I'm not alone. The desire to curl into a ball is so strong, I almost lose it. Gods, I thought Wolf was scary. He's nothing on this new vampire. I turn slowly and find Rylan standing in the doorway, watching me with those icy blue eyes. A quick glance over his shoulder confirms we're alone.

Great.

"Malachi seems to think you're something special." His tone conveys his doubt of *that* pretty damn clearly. Rylan steps into the room with exaggerated slowness. "You sent Wolf away. I'm surprised he listens to you."

"I've known Wolf a grand total of twenty-four hours and even I know he does what he wants, when he wants."

He raises a single eyebrow. "You don't know him. You don't know Malachi. You sure as fuck don't know me."

If he lifted his leg and peed to mark his territory, I wouldn't be surprised at this point. Fear is still threatening to clog my throat, but anger rises in steady waves, battling the chill I feel just from standing in the same room as this vampire. I narrow my eyes. "How long have you been harboring a sad, unrequited love for Malachi? Centuries? It's got to sting he's shacking up with a dhampir now."

He flinches, the tiniest of movements, one I would have missed if not for my dhampir senses. When Rylan speaks, it's with a dry tone that raises the small hairs on the back of my neck. "You're bold."

"I was doomed the second I was born." I force myself to shrug, as if the painful truth of the sentence means nothing. "If not you, then someone else. The fact that I've made it this long is, frankly, surprising. My father hates me."

"A likely story."

Anger is quickly surpassing fear. I glare. "Yes, you're right. Fathers who love their daughters definitely ship them off to Gothic mansions haunted by famished vampires to be a resident blood bank and womb. Totally."

I blink and he's in front of me. Holy shit, he's fast. I didn't even see him move. This close, it's strange to discover he's only a few inches taller than me. His suit shows off a great body, but he's not nearly as huge as his presence makes him seem.

Rylan's hand whips out and closes around my throat. "I don't care about your sad little life. I care about Malachi, and I care about Wolf."

"Quite the exhaustive list." Gods, why can't I stop talking back? It's like rage has hijacked what little verbal brakes I had. "Should I be impressed?"

He stares at me with something akin to surprise. "Do you want to die?"

"Not particularly."

His dark brows pull together in a frown. "Why are you baiting me?"

"I don't like you." When he keeps frowning at me like I'm a disgusting but vaguely interesting insect, I snarl. "Either rip out my throat or get the fuck off me."

"Malachi says you taste different." He's not talking to me. He almost sounds like he's thinking aloud, musing to himself. "But he's young. There's so much he doesn't know. I suppose there's one way to find out."

Comprehension dawns. "No. Don't you dare."

It's too late. Rylan shifts his hand from my throat to my hair and wrenches my head to the side. I jerk back, but the counter is in my way, and even if it wasn't, he's too strong. They're always too goddamn strong. He bites me, sinking his teeth into my throat. He tenses against me. "What *are* you?"

I don't get a chance to answer before he bites me again. His free hand lands on the counter next to my hip and he presses his entire body to mine. Instant pleasure hits me in a wave. I grit my teeth, trying to fight it. I don't want it from *him*. I refuse to orgasm as a result of this asshole's bite, bloodline vampire or no.

But, fuck, it's good. Each pull tingles through my body, a sensual touch that doesn't care if I like this vampire. Pleasure winds through me, tightening with each movement of his mouth. I find myself clutching the front of his suit with no memory of moving my hands. I bite down hard on my lip, but the pain only spikes the pleasure hotter.

It doesn't matter if I fight it. My body doesn't care about how I feel when it comes to this vampire. It's too good. *He* feels too good. Rylan grabs one of my legs and hitches it up around his hip, opening me just enough so he can shift between my thighs. It lines us up perfectly, and then his cock is there, pressing against where I suddenly need him.

I whimper as I orgasm, hating myself. Hating him.

He lifts his head slowly and blinks down at me. His eyes have bled to a pure silver that looks otherworldly. "I see."

"Get. Off. Me."

He licks his lips. Slowly, oh so slowly, he releases me and takes a step back, and then another. "You sent Wolf for birth control?"

I reach up with a shaking hand to press my neck where he bit me. Two perfect puncture wounds. At least he didn't tear the skin. I shudder. "It's a temporary fix."

He nods, expression still contemplative. "I see."

"Stop saying that!" My head feels a little woozy. I really shouldn't have gone so long without eating. Really shouldn't have spent the morning fucking and forgetting exactly how much danger I am in. "Either kill me or get out."

"You're going to collapse before you take two steps."

I'm not sure he's wrong, but that doesn't mean I'm going to lower myself to ask for help from *him*. I don't want him to touch me again. I don't... I try to push past him and the room turns into a sickening swirl of color and then goes black.

14

"SHE'S NOT HUMAN."

"Get the fuck out of here, Rylan."

I keep my eyes closed and maintain my slow breathing. I'm lying on a bed, and the lack of dust smells means it's likely Malachi's. I also don't seem to have acquired any new aches and pains, which means Rylan didn't let me face-plant in the kitchen. Honestly, I'm surprised. He seems the type to let me crumple and then leave me there for someone else to find. Or maybe just kick me a few times while I was down.

"Listen to me, you idiot. She might be half vampire, but her other half isn't entirely human."

What's he talking about? The ice has cracked in his voice and he sounds almost... Excited isn't the right word. Intense. Incredibly intense.

Malachi curses. "You've done enough, don't you think?"

"Mal—"

A low whistle. "I leave for an hour and look what trouble you two get into." Wolf. The crinkle of a plastic bag. "Did you kill her?" He sounds only mildly interested, and I might be hurt if I didn't recognize the question as so incredibly Wolf. He's pure chaos in motion. I'm honestly a little surprised he actually made it to the store and returned rather than wandering off to get into trouble elsewhere and reappearing in a few days—or a few years.

"He bit her." The accusation in Malachi's quiet statement is nearly enough to make me open my eyes.

"She's fine. She just needs to eat something."

"She's mortal."

"Not as mortal as you think."

There it is again. Rylan still hasn't elaborated on what the hell he's talking about. I finally give up and open my eyes. Malachi and Rylan stand over the bed, a bare six inches between them. They look half a second from fighting or fucking, and as I blink up at them, I'm honestly not sure which outcome is most likely. The intensity in the room makes it hard to breathe, or maybe that's because I'm so light-headed.

Wolf has a plastic bag dangling from one finger and looks distantly amused like he always seems to. He sees me first and crosses to drop the bag on the bed next to me. "I got what you asked for."

I leverage myself up to sit, ignoring the other two men for now. This is the priority. I dig out the pills and raise my eyebrows at the vanilla protein drink he also purchased. Not to mention the dozens of boxes of condoms in every variety and...flavor. "Huh."

"Covering all the bases, love." He plucks the pill package from my hand and opens it, but he hesitates when I reach for it. "Are you sure?"

"What is that?"

I don't look at Malachi. "We didn't use protection." We didn't even *talk* about using protection. Stuff like diseases might not be an issue—vampires heal everything, even that—but we should have been smarter when half the reason I'm here is because my father wants a little bloodline vampire baby to control. Reckless. So fucking reckless.

He catches Wolf's wrist and snags the box out of his hand. The more he reads, the harder he frowns. "What is this?"

"It's Plan B. It's a..." I wave my hand vaguely. "A concentrated form of birth control." I heard a group of the humans talking about it when they didn't think any of the vampires were around. No one in my father's compound used protection, but they were whispering about a way to avoid getting pregnant by the turned vampires. They all had their eyes set on the bloodline ones and didn't want a dhampir baby without any powers. None of them seemed to worry their *bloodline* dhampir child might not have powers. Another way I'm a freak, an eternal disappointment.

"Will this hurt you?"

I hadn't really thought about it. "No?" I honestly don't know. It's made for humans, and while my system seems to function nearly identically, there's really no telling. "I don't think so?"

"But you don't know."

I reach for it, but he holds it just beyond my grasp. "Malachi, give it here. Worst case, something goes wrong and you just give me blood to heal me. It's fine." I'm sure it's fine. I don't sound quite as confident as I want to, but I'm rattled and I can feel Rylan's gaze drilling a hole into the side of my head. I turn to him. "Tell him! This is what you want, isn't it?"

A muscle in Rylan's jaw twitches. "Have you taken human medication before?"

I blink. "Not you, too. You've been petitioning for my death since you showed up. What do you care?"

"Circumstances have changed."

I blink again. "Yeah, I'm going to need you to elaborate on what the hell you mean because you aren't making any sense."

Rylan crosses his arms over his chest. "You're not human."

"I'm dhampir."

He glares. "That's not what I'm talking about. These two don't recognize it because they're babies." He motions at Malachi and Wolf. "By the time they were born, we'd already started retreating and so dhampirs became more and more uncommon outside colonies like your fathers, places we don't go."

I'm still trying to comprehend how old Rylan must be if he's calling Malachi and Wolf *babies*. I'm still not quite sure how long they've been around, but it's long enough to get stuffy and mad, respectively. If I lined the three of them up, I'd assume Rylan was the youngest based on how he acts. Shows what I know.

Malachi's looking at Rylan with something other than antagonism. "What are you saying?"

"Who cares? Regardless of what I am, I have no magic to speak of, so it doesn't matter." I try to grab the box again. "*None* of this matters or has anything to do with the potential pregnancy."

"Ingesting chemicals the humans have thrown together is dangerous. There's no guarantee our blood would be enough to counteract it."

I am half a second from shrieking in frustration. "Then you get your wish and I'm dead. I still don't see why you're arguing."

Rylan leans down and looks at me. Silver flashes over his eyes and the sight of it holds me immobile despite my anger. "You really don't know, do you?"

"Rylan," Wolf drawls. "You're not usually such a tease. Spit it out and tell us what she is."

"I don't know."

Malachi curses and Wolf laughs. "All that buildup for nothing. Pity."

"If I knew what she was, this would be simpler to navigate." Rylan still hasn't taken his gaze from me. Finally, he shakes his head. "We can't risk it."

That's about enough of that. I start moving to the edge of the mattress. I can't let myself believe what he's saying. When I was young, I dreamed someday my magic would present itself and I'd be able to cast illusions like other dhampirs of my father's bloodline. Those dreams have long since turned to ash. It's not happening. Wanting it despite all evidence pointing to the contrary is a recipe for hating myself, and there are already enough people in this world who hate me. I don't need to add to their number. I'm not about to start now. "Yeah, you're still not making any sense, so I'm going to need that pill now."

Malachi tosses the box to Wolf and catches my shoulders. "Let's hear what he has to say." His expression is carefully neutral. "If, when he's done talking, you still want it, you can have it."

Frustration sinks its claws into me, but I do my best to stifle it. At least they're talking to me and no one has set the damn pill on fire or something, so I suppose that's progress. "Fine."

"And drink that." Wolf points at the protein drink. "You're looking peaky, love."

"Thanks," I say drily, but I *am* feeling dizzy still, so I make myself open the bottle and take a few drinks. It's warm and less than appetizing, but it's better than nothing. I twist to look at Rylan. "It doesn't matter what other theoretical supernatural blood I carry because I have no magic. I'm not even particularly strong or fast for a dhampir. I am utterly average in every way, aside from apparently being particularly tasty."

Instead of answering, he moves back to lean against the wall and studies me. "What do you know about other supernatural creatures?"

Little more than rumors. My father is so hyperfocused on vampires, he doesn't care about the other things out there that aren't human. Why would he? They don't bother him, they can't help him accomplish his goals, and so they're beneath his notice. "Next to nothing. Other than apparently some of them would be strong enough to break the blood ward." Understanding dawns. I frown. "But again, for the millionth time, I have no magic. I can't break a blood ward. I wouldn't even know how to try." And I don't want to try. Not when it won't change anything. I spent countless hours focusing so hard I got piercing headaches because I was sure if I just focused hard enough, I could manifest my magic. It didn't work then. It won't work now.

"Some of them mature late. A quarter century is nothing."

My chest gets tight and I have to fight to speak through it without yelling. "Stop it."

His brows draw together and he looks actually confused instead of just icy and terrifying. "I don't understand why you're fighting this. It's a fact. Your blood is not just vampire and human. There's something else there. It's familiar, but I can't place it. The fact that it's strong enough to be tasted means it's strong enough to manifest." He tilts his head to the side. "It would explain your lack of magic. The other blood is more powerful than the vampire half of you."

"You're crazy."

His blue eyes are merciless. "Why not try? What do you have to lose?"

I close my eyes and strive to think instead of reacting emotionally. It will hurt if this is all bullshit and nothing changes. It will hurt a lot. But it won't kill me. If I don't get out of this house, if *Malachi* doesn't get out of this house, my father might.

Really, it's a simple decision when I lay it out like that.

I exhale slowly and open my eyes. "What do I have to do?"

Rylan glances at Wolf and Malachi and then refocuses on me. "There are two ways. Pain or pleasure."

I wait, but he doesn't offer anything more. "So you want to torture me."

Malachi snorts. "No, little dhampir, no one is getting tortured."

"It might be the only answer." I glance at him, and gods, my chest aches just looking at him. It's too soon to feel something so strong, but hell if I can push the feeling away. "I've *had* pleasure since I've been here, especially in the last twelve hours. Nothing's happened."

"Pleasure." Wolf drops onto the bed beside me and laughs in that slightly unhinged way of his. "You haven't seen anything yet, love." He grins, flashing fang. "But it'll be fun to blow that pretty little mind of yours."

I had already planned on grabbing every bit of pleasure possible, so I suppose this isn't exactly a trial. Still... I look over to find Rylan still watching me too closely. Every instinct I have says the other shoe is about to drop. "What am I missing?"

"Those two can't do it on their own." He doesn't move, doesn't seem to breathe. "I have to be involved."

I blink. "You wanted me dead—literally dead—twenty minutes ago."

"Things change."

"You don't like me."

His lips twitch the tiniest bit. "Are you really that naive you think sex and fondness have anything to do with each other?"

No, of course not. But there is a large distance between *fondness* and wanting to murder someone. Isn't there? "No. I guess I'm not." I guess if he can handle his side of things, all he has to do is bite me to get me on board.

And Rylan is sexy. I really hate that he's sexy. He's like some ice king that's wandered in and letting him touch me might freeze me right down to my bones, but I can't quite forget how good it felt to have him pressed against me.

Apparently now I've gotten a taste for sex and bloodline vampire bites, I'm in danger of getting addicted. The thought should worry me, but I'll deal with the consequences later. If there's a way to get us out of this trap my father's constructed, I'm going to do it.

I look up at Malachi. He doesn't seem particularly pleased by this turn of events, but he's not exactly *dis*pleased, either. I can't read the expression on his face. He motions to the box in his hand. "Will you agree to hold off on this until we try?"

"The longer I hold off, the less effective it is."

"All the same."

I search his face, but it's like the first few days here. I can't tell what he's thinking. "If this works, you'll be free." He'll have no reason to keep me around.

That should make me happy, right? After all, the only thing I want is what I've wanted since I was old enough to watch my hopes turn to ash. Freedom. No vampires to speak of. A chance to figure out my own way. And hopefully not stumble right into a government facility that will spend the rest of my life doing experiments on me.

I drop my gaze, but Malachi plants his hand on the bed and leans down until it's more awkward to avoid his gaze than to look at him. I still can't read the expression on his face. "We won't leave you hanging."

Something like hope flutters in my chest and I want nothing more than to squash it. "You've been locked up here a long time, Malachi. You're not in any position to offer me protection." Which isn't what he's offering anyway. He said they won't leave me hanging. *They*. I shake my head. "And you can't speak for them."

"No, I can't." He doesn't move. "But I'm speaking for me. I want you to stay with me. If that's not what you want, we'll figure out a way for you to land safely. I give you my word."

There's no reason to trust him. We've known each other a tiny fraction of a moment and he might be a liar in addition to everything else. I can't help trusting him all the same. "Okay," I whisper.

"Okay?"

Gods, why does he always make me say it? I know, though, don't I? "Okay, let's try this."

15

I EXPECT US TO GET RIGHT DOWN TO BUSINESS, BUT apparently that's not the plan. Rylan leaves, muttering something about preparations. Wolf plants a devastating kiss on my mouth and then he leaves, too. They couldn't be more obvious if they'd hand painted a sign saying *We'll give you two time to talk*.

Malachi holds out his hand. "Let's go find you something to eat."

I'm starving, but I'm so nervous, I don't know if I can eat. It's more than the sex that has my stomach tying itself in knots. They're putting a lot of hope in something that's barely more than a theory. "This might not work."

He tugs me off the bed and across the room to the door. "If it doesn't, we'll figure out something else."

How can he be so calm at a moment like this? His very

freedom is on the line. "Malachi…" I dig in my heels a little and he slows to a stop. "You're just going to do this on Rylan's say-so? The longer we put off me taking that pill, the less likely it is to work." I don't know what the odds are that I'm pregnant. I know how cycles work in theory, but I hardly track mine closely enough to tell if I'm ovulating right now or in the near future. And really, all my information is related to full humans. I don't know how a dhampir's reproductive system might differ, especially when there are vampires and magic involved.

I don't know if the damn pill would work even if we use it under the best case circumstances.

"Mina."

Gods, I love it when he says my name. It's like I'm a tuning fork thrumming just from the sound. "I'm not being unreasonable."

"I know." He gives my hand a squeeze and pulls me closer so he can wrap his big arms around me. I have absolutely no business feeling safe right now just because he's holding me. The list of things to worry about is longer than my arm and seems to be growing by the minute. A hug doesn't solve anything.

It feels really, really good, though.

I close my eyes and relax against him. "If this doesn't work, Rylan is going to start in about killing me again."

"No one is killing you."

"If not me then some innocent human Wolf snatches up. Better to be me." It's not that I want to die. The exact opposite is true. But I don't know if I can live with myself if someone innocent dies in my place. Being that ruthless would make me no better than my father. It would make me a monster.

"Mina." Malachi digs his hands into my hair and tugs until I lift my face to his. "Rylan is very, very old. He's also not in the habit of spouting off the way Wolf likes to. If he says this can be done, he's likely right."

"You don't seem to like him very much."

"Our history is…"

"Complicated?"

His lips curve. "Complicated."

There seems to be a lot of that going around. I sigh. "A lot has changed in a little over a week. It seems like it's too much, too fast. I shouldn't feel—" I barely manage to cut myself off before I say something I can't take back. Like confess I've gone and done the unforgivable. I *like* Malachi, even when I find him infuriating. I might even be falling for him, though it's not like I have much experience with that sort of thing.

"I feel it, too." He brushes his thumbs over my cheekbones. "When you've lived as long as I have, you learn not to question these things. Some feelings transcend logic."

"That's just it. I'm not going to live as long as you, not by any stretch of the imagination."

"Trust Rylan."

I snort. "Yeah, he was calling for my head not too long ago, and then he pulled a full one-eighty between one bite and the next. Trust takes longer to build."

"Then trust me."

I open my mouth to repeat what I just said. Trust takes longer to build. But the truth is I *do* trust Malachi. Not only do I trust him not to hurt me, but I trust him to keep his word. It's a little disconcerting, to be perfectly honest. I've spent this long relying only on myself and the only truth that held steady was I couldn't trust anyone.

I take an unsteady breath. "I do trust you. Even if I shouldn't."

The smile Malachi gives me is nothing like I've seen before. It's a small smile, but it lights up his dark eyes with something akin to happiness. "We'll get free, Mina."

I kiss him. It's not even a decision. I simply hook his neck and go onto my toes as I pull him down to me. He comes more than willingly. The second our lips touch, it's as if an inferno lights inside me. I need more. I dig my hands into his hair and Malachi hooks the back of my thighs and lifts me so I can wrap my legs around his waist. One step and my back meets the wall. Gods, this man is addicting in a way I don't know if I'll ever have a defense against. I don't know if I want one.

He kisses me like I'm the best thing he's ever tasted. Like he'll never get enough. We devolve into tongue and teeth and little sounds that mean everything and nothing.

Malachi pulls back a bare inch. "You need to eat."

"Later." I'm already reaching between us to push at the waistband of his lounge pants. "I need you more."

He curses, the sounds sweet against my lips. "You're hell on my self-control."

"Sorry?" I delve into his pants and wrap my fist around his cock. The feeling of him pulsing against my palm has my whole body clenching. I need him and I need him now. "Please. I'll make it quick."

He gives one of those rough laughs. "I think that's supposed to be my line." But he leans back enough that I can push his pants down and free his cock. I start to guide him to my entrance and then hesitate. "We're supposed to be using condoms, I think?"

He's breathing as hard as I am. For a moment, I think he might argue, but he finally gives himself a rough shake. "They're too far away."

I don't have a chance to argue. He shifts his grip and sinks to his knees before me, holding me aloft as if I weigh nothing at all. I yelp a little. "Malachi, I want your cock."

"Too bad. You get my tongue." And then his mouth is on my pussy and I forget everything but the slick feel of him licking me to orgasm. It feels so fucking good I never want it to stop. He's not rushing, either. He's licking me like he relishes my taste, this moment, as much as I do. Under his tongue, my body coils tighter and tighter with pleasure, ascending toward a peak that will send me hurtling into oblivion.

I'm gasping. I think I'm speaking, but I can't make out the words. It seems beyond comprehension that he can do this to me without biting me. That there are no vampire tricks or magic involved. Just Malachi's overwhelming strength and the desire weaving a spell around us.

I barely register we're in the hallway until I look up and realize we aren't alone any longer. Rylan and Wolf stand at the top of the stairs, watching us with identical looks of lust in their eyes. Wolf's have bled pure crimson. Rylan's only flash silver, but there's no animosity in the way he looks at me now. No, there's pure need.

It's too late to wonder how I feel about that. I'm too far

gone. I dig my hands into Malachi's long hair and roll my hips, grinding myself against his mouth and tongue as I come. He bites me, sending my orgasm to new heights. I scream and slam back against the wall, damn near convulsing with the sheer amount of pleasure pouring through me.

He gives my pussy one last long lick and then rises easily to resume the position we started in. He looks down at me with eyes gone pure black. For a moment, I'm sure he'll fuck me right here, condom or no. I almost hope he does. Even after coming so hard, I crave the feel of him inside me.

But he just turns with me still in his arms and stalks down the hall to the stairs. Rylan and Wolf edge out of the way as he carries me down to the kitchen and sets me on the counter. I blink and weave a little. "I thought..."

"Food, Mina. Or you're going to pass out before we get to the good stuff."

What we just did *was* the good stuff. What we did this morning and last night was good stuff. I can't quite comprehend how it can get better than *that*.

Rylan and Wolf walk through the door a bare second later. Wolf veers toward the fridge and Malachi, but Rylan walks to me. Without so much as a word, he flicks up my shirt and looks at my pussy. "He bit you. You need blood."

"I'm fine." I don't know why I'm arguing. I also don't know why I flash hot at the hungry way he looks at me before he lets the shirt drop. "And *you* bit me first."

He doesn't respond other than to lift his wrist to his mouth and bite down. It's not a polite little bite. No, he rips his own flesh as if it's nothing. As if he doesn't feel the pain. Rylan grabs the back of my head and lifts his wrist to my mouth. "Quickly, before it heals."

I want to argue. I do. But his blood makes my fangs ache so intensely, I could weep from the sensation. Even as I tell myself I'll only have a taste, I cover his wound with my mouth. When I took Malachi's blood, it felt like lightning shooting into my body.

If Malachi's blood is lightning, Rylan's is a hurricane.

The taste of it explodes on my tongue and I swear every hair on my body stands at end as if I've stuck my finger in a light socket—except a thousand times more powerful. I whimper but I don't know if it's in pain or pleasure. I can actually feel the blood moving through me, down my throat, into my stomach, the magic there shooting out to the tips of my fingers and toes.

And then it stops.

I drag my tongue over his newly healed skin, and I've almost lost myself enough to start gnawing on him like a goddamn animal.

"That's enough."

I blink my eyes open and stare at him. He was dangerously handsome before, but now he's reached another level. The entire room has. It feels like I'm seeing a new level of detail my eyes couldn't discern before. I look at Wolf and Malachi and they practically crackle with energy, though it looks different on them than it does on Rylan. In fact, it looks different for each of them. I lick my lips, tasting Rylan's blood. "How old are you?"

"It's considered rude to ask."

I finally look back at him. After he bit me earlier, I was feeling woozy and exhausted. Now, I feel like I could run a record-breaking marathon. "Even Malachi's blood didn't make me feel like this."

"Like I said, he's a baby." He releases me slowly and steps back. When he speaks, it's aimed at Malachi. "We will go over what breaking the ward entails while she eats."

I slide off the counter and bounce on my toes a little. Yeah, I feel better than great. I belatedly realize my knee doesn't ache; it hasn't today at all. It's probably a good thing Rylan doesn't like me that much because I could get addicted to drinking his blood. I give myself a little shake. My thoughts are buzzing at twice their speed and I'm having trouble focusing. "I'm not hungry anymore."

"All the same, you need to eat." Malachi sets a plate with a sandwich on the table and points at the chair for me to sit. Two glasses join it, one with water, one with orange juice.

I make a face, but I know he's right so I sit down. My stomach chooses that moment to growl, so I pick up half of the sandwich and obediently start to eat. The vampires take up positions on the other three sides of the table. Rylan plants his elbows on the table. "The goal is to fill the blood ward with so much power that it bursts."

I take another bite of sandwich to avoid pointing out I don't actually have power. It'll just start an argument, and I suspect the only way they'll believe me is if we go through with this. And if it works...

No.

Easier to shut down that thought before something as

unforgivable as hope can take root. I told Malachi I trusted him to not drop me like yesterday's trash the second he gets free, but that's as far as I can stretch this new trust. Letting in that old hope, the fragile belief that maybe I *am* special... It's too dangerous. I don't know if I'll recover from it when this invariably fails after I let myself believe it'll succeed.

As if he can hear my thoughts, Rylan shoots me a sharp look, but he keeps going. "We do that by boosting Mina's power with our blood and then making her come so hard, it overrides the blocks in her mind."

I blink. "What?" He said pain or pleasure could do the trick, but I didn't really think about what it would entail. "Why do we need all three of you to make that happen?"

Wolf laughs. "Three cocks are better than one, love. Trust us. You'll have a good time."

Even when I had sex with both Wolf and Malachi, it wasn't at the same time. Adding in Rylan? I shiver. "That seems like it's going to be overwhelming."

"That's the idea." Rylan's cold gaze flicks over me.

Malachi has that strange look on his face again, the one I'm not sure how to define. I can't tell if he's looking forward to this or dreading it or something infinitely more complicated. "You'll enjoy yourself. Trust me."

There it is again. That demand that I trust him. I take a tiny sip of water, but it does nothing to combat the closed feeling in my throat. "I do."

16

THROUGH SOME UNSPOKEN DECISION, THE MEN DECIDE tonight is the best time to do this—I hesitate to call it a ritual. But I'm not sure what other word applies. Rylan leaves again, though this time he gives no information about where he's headed.

I'm not sure how I end up back in Malachi's room. I had every intention of going back to mine, but it seems like I blink and the last few days start catching up with me. And then I'm on the bed, sandwiched between Wolf and Malachi, and my eyelids feel like someone's attached weights to them. "I should..."

"Rest." Malachi smooths my hair back from my temple. "We have a few hours."

Even as I know I'm not going to win this fight with sleep, I keep trying. "My things..."

"I'll get them packed." His lips brush my forehead. "Sleep, Mina. We'll wake you when it's time."

It feels like one moment I'm trying to form words to argue and the next a hand on my shoulder is shaking me gently awake. I open my eyes and squint at the darkness coating the room. It was late morning when I fell asleep. "What time is it?"

"It's almost time to begin."

I sit up. Malachi is on the bed next to me. Wolf and Rylan are talking softly on the other side of the room. It's happening. It's really happening. Something like panic flutters in my throat. "I need a shower. To brush my teeth."

"Be quick."

I slip out of the room before they can argue. As promised, my suitcase is sitting on my bed, packed nearly identically to how I originally had it. Despite everything, I smile a little. "Pushy vampire." I grab the stuff I need and take a quick shower and brush my teeth. Though I'd hoped the time would give me a moment to calm down, being away from them has panic bleating even louder.

This isn't going to work.

I don't care how old Rylan is, how knowledgeable, how much the other two seem to trust him. If I had some hidden power, I would have brought it forth before now out of sheer desperation. I wanted it *so* badly; surely if it existed, it would have appeared before now?

I stare down at my suitcase. Am I supposed to get dressed again? We're just going to end up naked, right? It seems weird to put on clothes, but it seems even weirder to just walk in there without anything on me at all.

After calling myself seven different kinds of fool, I pull out a short, thin robe and shrug into it. It's as close to a reasonable compromise as I can come up with, but I still feel incredibly vulnerable as I pad back to Malachi's room.

They've turned off the lights and added a scattering of candles around the perimeter of the room. I don't know if it's meant to be romantic, but it feels like I'm about to play sacrifice in some kind of arcane ritual. All three of the men wear lounge pants and nothing else. Apparently they were as hesitant to start out naked as I was.

All three of their attentions narrow on me as I step into the room and softly shut the door behind me. It feels different than it has up to this point. I am painfully aware this trio are apex predators and I am one measly step above human.

I might not survive the night.

They're going to have to be very, very careful to ensure I do.

The thought has a borderline hysterical laugh bubbling up, but I clamp my jaw shut to keep it inside. Malachi crosses to me, and I appreciate he's walking human-slow instead of blurring. I don't think my nerves can handle being startled right now.

He takes my shoulders and smooths his thumbs over my collarbones. "Rylan says condoms will affect things."

I blink. Of all the things I expected, that wasn't on the list. "What?"

"There's magic even in our semen," Rylan says from his spot next to the window. "It can't hurt to add it in, along with the blood."

I blink again. "That sounds like one hell of a line."

Did he smile? It's hard to say. Wolf nudges him with his shoulder. "You're playing fast and loose, old friend."

"No, I'm not."

Wolf laughs. "Whatever you have to tell yourself." He turns to me. His eyes are already crimson and his smile is more than a little deranged. "You ready, love?"

No. I'm not even close to ready.

Malachi steps between me and the other vampires. "Breathe, Mina."

"I'm breathing." I sound more like I'm wheezing. This is a mess. How am I supposed to get to some point of magical orgasm-to-end-all-orgasms when I feel so skittish, I'm half a second from turning around and running out of this room like my hair is on fire? I look up at Malachi. "Bite me?"

His eyes widen just a fraction and it's as if my nerves trigger something in him. The strange expression he's been wearing since Rylan showed up disappears and he gives me a slow smile. "Where's the fun in that, little dhampir?"

It seems like it's been forever since he called me that, but I can't help leaning toward him in response. "This isn't fun. This is serious."

"I'm going to kiss you now." He makes no move to close the distance between us farther. "And then Wolf is going to touch you. And then Rylan. Okay?"

Is he asking permission *now*? I've already agreed to this. There's no reason to walk me through this like I'm an innocent. Except I *am* damn near an innocent when it comes to this kind of stuff. Having sex a handful of times does not prepare one for whatever this is supposed to be. "Okay," I say softly.

"If at any point you want to stop, we stop."

Behind him, Wolf laughs. "She won't want to stop once we get going."

Malachi ignores him. "Do you understand?"

Does *he* understand by constantly putting this in my hands, he's stripping me of the ability to fully let go? I can't pretend I'm just a butterfly being swept along before a gale-force wind, praying that it doesn't rip me to pieces. It's so much easier when you don't have a choice, and Malachi insists on giving me one, over and over again. I kind of hate him for it. I kind of love him for it, too.

I take a shaky breath. "Yes, I understand."

Instead of pressing me further, he leans down and brushes a light kiss to my lips. And then another one. I'm so tense, a soft touch might make me shatter, but the third kiss comes with a hint of his teeth against my bottom lip. I jump and the motion presses me to his chest. He wraps his arms around me, and I relax into what's becoming a familiar sensation of being held by Malachi. He's so fucking *big*. He makes me feel weirdly fragile in a way that isn't entirely unpleasant. Maybe it's because he's so careful with me, careful with our respective differences in strength. I don't know. I just know I whimper against his mouth and slide my hands up his chest.

That's when I feel Wolf behind me, lifting my hair off my neck. His lips are cool as he kisses the newly exposed skin, and I shiver when his fangs lightly scrape me. Malachi shifts his arms a little and then Wolf's gripping my hips in the newly created space. They buoy me between them until I feel pleasantly dizzy from Malachi's drugging kisses and Wolf playing with the sensitive skin at the base of my neck.

Malachi tenses and the scent of blood teases me. He breaks our kiss and leans his head to the side, baring his neck. I catch sight of a long cut and of Rylan behind him, holding a knife. It's almost enough to jar me out of my pleasure-soaked state, but Wolf uses his body to press me closer to Malachi, uses his mouth on the back of my neck to guide me to the fresh cut.

I moan at the first taste. Rylan's blood might be more powerful, but I don't think I'll ever get tired of the way Malachi's zings through me. I drink from him until the cut closes and then I can't quite help giving his skin one last lick. It feels like my nerve endings are sparking and I lean up to try to catch Malachi's mouth.

He turns me in his arms and then Wolf's there. He kisses me before I can fully register they're moving me around like a toy between them. Malachi coasts his hands over my sides and around to my stomach. He cups my breasts through my robe, lightly pinching my nipples.

I moan against Wolf's mouth and his fingers clench harder onto my hips. Not hard enough to really hurt, but the faint ache grounds me in a way I desperately need. I nip his bottom lip the same way Malachi did to mine, enjoying how he jerks a little in response.

For the first time since Rylan put forth this plan, the nerves settle a little. It will be okay. As long as we keep touching, everything will be okay.

Malachi traces the opening of my robe, tugging it until it falls open. As if they planned this, Wolf kisses his way down my neck to my newly bared breasts. He makes a sound of appreciation and then he pulls one nipple into his mouth while Malachi keeps up that delicious light pinching with the other. I stare down at the sight of Wolf's mouth on me, of Malachi's hands on me at the same time. It's just like before, when they drove me to orgasm together, and yet it's entirely different.

I never want it to stop.

Movement behind Wolf draws my attention. Rylan sits on the bed, idly toying with the knife in his hand, his attention entirely on us, his eyes fully silver. I tense, but Malachi uses his free hand to cup my jaw and urge me to bend backward so he can kiss me again. I know it's a distraction technique, but I eagerly arch to accept his mouth.

Wolf uses his mouth to keep parting my robe until he gets to the tie and yanks it open. The blood pounds through my body, but I don't think he's to blame. It's this situation, it's Malachi's blood inside me, still sizzling through my veins. The feeling has settled a little, as if I've absorbed it. It must be what's happened before, but I've never felt the transition as acutely as I do right now. "More."

Both men pause. Malachi lets out a slow breath. Wolf looks up at me and grins, flashing fang. "You heard the lady."

Malachi moves first, pulling the robe off my shoulders and tossing it aside. He lifts me into his arms and starts for the bed.

Wolf snorts. "Things were just getting interesting."

"You can have your turn later." Malachi sets me on the bed on the opposite side from Rylan, and there's no way it's coincidence. I'm still uneasy about Rylan, and even more off-center because of my reaction to him. I don't like him, but I can't deny part of me is drawn to him. It's uncomfortable and I don't like it, but ultimately he's right. This is just sex, and the purpose of it tonight is to somehow awaken my theoretical magic. The orgasms are just a convenient side effect.

Better this than torture.

Malachi nudges me onto my back and moves down my body to wedge himself between my legs. He went down on me in the kitchen and again in the hallway, but somehow this feels a thousand times more intimate. His broad shoulders force my thighs wide and the way he looks at me...

I shiver and lick my lips. "Please."

Wolf drops down next to me, planting himself between us and the edge of the bed. He grins at Malachi. "You stole my turn and now you're teasing. Rude."

Malachi presses an openmouthed kiss to my thigh. "You can have a turn later."

There it is again. That feeling of being a toy between them, something to be passed around. I expect to hate it, but the feeling never comes. How can it when they're being so careful with me? Not a toy after all. A *treat*. I shiver.

Malachi drags his tongue over my pussy and the fire behind him flares higher. Wolf tenses. "Keep it locked down."

"Mmm." Malachi ignores the other man and keeps licking me. It's not like before in the hallway. He's taking his time. It feels so fucking good, but the feeling he's savoring every little taste? It only makes this hotter.

I try to roll my hips, to guide him up to my clit, but he uses one arm to pin my lower half to the bed without missing a beat. I moan. I can't help it. Desire drugs my senses, and a hot, hard knot starts to pulse inside me. Close. I'm so close.

Malachi chooses that moment to slow his kisses until they're the barest brushing of his lips to my heated flesh. Nowhere near enough to get me off. "Please!"

Wolf traces a lazy finger up my stomach and between my breasts. "We're just getting started, love. Don't get impatient." His crimson eyes flick to the other side of me. "Now."

I follow his gaze and tense. I was so focused on Malachi, I hadn't realized Rylan now lay on the other side of me. He reaches over my chest and takes Wolf's wrist. The knife flashes and a wide cut opens on Wolf's forearm. Rylan holds my gaze as he guides Wolf's bleeding arm to my mouth. "Drink deeply."

I obey without thinking. Wolf's blood is like drinking pure fire. I might find that ironic later. Maybe. Right now, it's yet another sensation on the heels of so much. The lightning from Malachi isn't completely gone and the fire dances with it, sending shivers through me. I gasp, belatedly realizing Wolf's wound has healed. I start to look at him, but he's already moved down to my breasts again. He pulls one nipple into his mouth as Malachi shoves his tongue inside me.

The dual sensations bow my back. "Oh gods."

I reach for Wolf, but Rylan catches my wrists and presses them back to the bed. It causes him to loom over me, and I might be out of my mind, but I swear his gaze drops to my mouth for a long moment before he drags it back to my eyes. "I'm going to touch you now."

It takes two tries to form words. "You're touching me right now."

"Not like this."

Malachi swirls his tongue around my clit and I have to close my eyes for a long moment. When I finally drag them open again, Rylan is still bent over me. Waiting for permission, I realize. I've already agreed to this, to all of it, but I nod slowly. "Okay."

I don't know what to expect. Most of my body is covered with Wolf and Malachi right now. There isn't much space left for Rylan. But he surprises the hell out of me when he leans down and kisses me.

Just like that, everything changes.

17

MALACHI KEEPS LICKING MY PUSSY AS IF HE'LL NEVER get enough, but every time I get close to the edge, he retreats. It's agonizing. It's glorious. Wolf lavishes my breasts with attention, but it's as if he and Malachi can communicate without words. Every time Malachi backs off, Wolf does the same, gentling his nips and kisses to almost nothing.

And Rylan?

Rylan kisses me like he never needs to breathe. The slow slide of his tongue against mine mimics Malachi's against my clit, almost perfectly in sync. It's so good and nowhere near enough.

They overwhelm me, moving with such synchronization, it's as if they've done this before. Maybe they have. And through it all, Malachi's and Wolf's powers thrum through me, making me feel weightless and yet all too present in my body. I have the frenzied thought that I could fly, just levitate directly off this bed and shoot out the window to dance with the stars.

Malachi brings me to the edge again and lifts his head. I fight against Rylan's hold, fight to reach for Malachi and force him back to my aching pussy. I arch back, breaking the kiss the tiniest amount. "Please." My voice is rough and I'm damn near sobbing. "Please, no more."

The vampires pause. Wolf drags his mouth along the underside of my breast. "Dibs on her ass."

"*What?*"

But they aren't listening. Rylan shifts back, using his grip on my wrists to pull me up from the bed. Malachi rolls onto his back, taking me with him, and I end up perched above his face with Rylan kneeling in front of me. I blink at them. "Um."

"Trust me." Malachi gives my pussy one last thorough kiss and then retreats.

The mattress dips as Wolf moves to my back and Rylan releases one hand to press it between my shoulder blades, easing me down until my face presses against the mattress. The new position leaves my ass in the air, leaves me completely vulnerable, but I can't bring myself to care. My body pulses in time with my heartbeat. I'm so wound up, it won't take much to shove me over the edge. I've never been denied like this, never been *played with* like this.

I think I love it.

Something cool and wet spreads down my ass, and I barely have a chance to understand what's happening when a hard cock presses to that tight entrance. I tense. I can't help it. "Wait."

Wolf—because it is Wolf at my back—hesitates. "Relax, love."

Yeah, not likely. I start to lift my head, but Rylan shifts his hand to my hair. I tense further, expecting... I'm not sure what I expect. It's not for him to run his fingers through my hair. It feels good, almost like comfort, but surely I'm misunderstanding. He keeps doing it and gentles his grip on my wrist. "Breathe, Mina. Relax. Let him in."

I take a breath, and then another. Slowly, oh so slowly, my muscles relax one by one. Wolf strokes my hips, my ass, the small of my back. "That's it, love. Let me in." He eases a little more into me.

I'm not sure if I expect pain, but it's more of a strange fullness. Nothing like when he and Malachi fucked my pussy. But not unpleasant. I take another breath and relax completely, giving myself over to this.

Rylan keeps stroking my hair, Wolf keeps touching me, keeps murmuring meaningless words in a low voice as he works his cock farther and farther into my ass. And then his hips meet mine and he exhales harshly. "Fuck, that feels good."

"Hold it together." This from Malachi.

I turn my head to find him kneeling on the other side, watching us with fire in his eyes. Behind him, the flames remain safely in the fireplace but they've flared so high, they fill the space completely. How much of that is from when he ate my pussy and how much is from watching Wolf's cock sink into my ass? I don't know if I care.

"We're moving, love." Wolf bands an arm around my hips and rolls carefully onto his back, taking me with him. It makes him shift inside me, and I can't stop myself from whimpering. Wolf kisses my temple. "Does it hurt?"

"No," I gasp.

Malachi moves to kneel between my thighs. His cock looks even bigger than it did this morning, and I lick my lips as I stare at it. It couldn't be clearer what their plans are, and I'm not sure I'm going to survive it. I'm not sure I care. I glance at Rylan and frown. "What—"

"Not yet."

Malachi braces one hand beside me and Wolf and wraps a fist around his cock. He drags his blunt head through my folds and up to circle my clit. I whimper and writhe, but Wolf grabs my hips and forces me still. His breath is harsh against my temple. "It feels too good when you do that."

"Thought you could go for days," Malachi says, but he's too focused on the sight of his cock rubbing my pussy for the comment to sting. He notches himself at my entrance and then he's pressing in, in, in.

I can't breathe.

It's too much. I'm too full. They're too big.

I open my mouth to tell them that, to beg them to... I don't even know. Hurry up? Stop? Something.

Rylan kisses me before I can give the words voice. He devours my whimpers and pleas as Malachi works his thick cock into me in short, steady strokes. I think I'm sobbing. I don't know. The sensations are so intense, it feels like I'm floating above my body, watching the scene play out. Malachi's muscles flex as he works himself into me until he's fully sheathed. And then he goes still, aside from the little tremors that shake his body.

Only then does Rylan lift his head. He moves back enough

to grab the knife and use it to slice a deep cut into his forearm, deeper than he cut Wolf or Malachi. He looks at Malachi as he presses his forearm to my mouth. "Now."

Malachi moves the moment Rylan's blood hits my tongue. He begins to fuck me in slow, deep thrusts, never quite pulling out all the way before he drives into me again. Beneath me, Wolf doesn't move, but he doesn't have to. His cock fills me, adding to the sensation every time Malachi thrusts deep. And the power of Rylan's blood surges through me, until it feels like my hair is floating around me.

Except...my hair *is* floating.

And so is Malachi's.

I can't see Wolf, and Rylan's hair is too short to tell, but there's a weightless feeling to the room, as if we've somehow decreased the force of gravity. But that's impossible. No, this is magic. I can *feel* it thrumming inside me in time with Malachi's thrusts. So close to the surface, but not there yet. Something...

Something's holding it back.

I'm holding it back.

I claw at Malachi's shoulders. "I need more." His brows draw together as he looks down at me and then he glances at Rylan. I follow his gaze. Desperation claws its way through me and I find myself reaching out to Rylan. "It's not enough. I need more. I can't let go."

Rylan hesitates. "If—"

"Fuck my mouth." Under different circumstances, I might enjoy the way his eyes blaze even brighter as shock suffuses his handsome face. Right now, I'm too intensely focused on that feeling of *almost*. I nod to myself. "Yes, that's what I need." If he does that, it will overwhelm me, I'm sure of it. Then maybe this horrible feeling of being almost there will burst. I glare up when I realize Rylan is still hesitating. "*Now*. Hurry."

He curses, but then he's shoving out of his pants and moving to kneel over us. It's a little awkward, but I don't care. I wrap my fist around Rylan's cock and reach for Malachi with my other hand. "Don't stop."

Malachi's expression is almost feral. "I won't."

I arch up and tug on Rylan's cock at the same time, guiding him into my mouth. He's not quite as long as Malachi and Wolf, but he's thicker, thick enough I have to work to suck him down. His low curse has me clenching around Malachi, but it's not enough. I can't get him deep enough.

Rylan, thank the gods, seems to understand. He touches my jaw. "Relax. Let me do the work."

Yes, that's what I need. I make a sound of assent and give myself over to all of them. Malachi smooths his hands up my thighs, pressing them up and out, splaying me open. "Her clit, Wolf." As Wolf snakes his hand around my hip to stroke my clit, Malachi picks up his pace until he's pounding into me. Rylan doesn't take quite as punishing a pace or depth, but as he starts fucking my face, I have to relax completely and let him lead. I have to submit. I have to become a receptacle for their bodies, for my pleasure. Wolf's clever fingers stroke my clit. This time, they aren't backing off. All four of us are cascading toward one inevitable ending.

The feeling inside me rushes higher, pressing against something invisible holding it in place. With each thrust, it surges. Again and again. Higher and higher. More and more.

Something tears deep in my soul as it ascends. It feels like someone shoved their hand into my chest and wrapped it around my bloody heart, squeezing, squeezing, squeezing until it bursts from my chest in a rush that has me crying out around Rylan's cock.

Glass shatters. A great pressure pushes against my skin. In the distance, I think I hear screaming.

And then Rylan curses and he's coming down my throat. I drink him down without thought, sucking on his cock even as he begins to ease away. Malachi shudders between my thighs and then he fills me in great spurts that have me moaning. Holy shit, what is happening? He barely moves out of the way before Wolf flips us, pinning me to the bed as he drives into me. I'm too loose to do anything but take it, and I have the distant thought that even this feels amazing. He pulls out a bare second before he comes across my back and then he slumps down beside me.

For a long moment, only the sound of our ragged breathing filled the room.

Then Malachi gives a choked laugh. "It worked. It fucking worked." He pulls me up and kisses me hard. "You did it, Mina."

I barely have the strength to cling to his shoulders as he pulls me into his arms and grabs someone's shirt to wipe down my back. "Are you sure?"

"Yes. The blood ward is gone."

Wolf stretches and his fingers feather along my thigh. "He'll have felt the rebound of it shattering. It'll put him out of commission for at least a few hours."

Him. My father.

I shiver in Malachi's arms. My body doesn't feel like my own. My skin is so sensitive I simultaneously want to shove him away and also rub myself all over him. "I don't think I can walk."

"You just got fucked to within an inch of your life. No shit you can't walk." Wolf laughs. "That was work well done, if I do say so myself."

"Malachi." For the first time since I met him, Rylan sounds... shocked. "Do you recognize what she is?"

I twist to look at Rylan. His eyes are still blazing silver and he's staring at me like I'm a poisonous snake that just slithered into his bed. It stings, but I try to rationalize my response; it's not as if he liked me to begin with. I take a shaky breath. "What am I?"

"Seraph," he says the word like a curse.

"A *seraph*?" Wolf throws himself onto his back and laughs so hard he has to clutch his stomach. "Our little dhampir is a fucking *angel*."

Seraph.

Malachi's arms tighten around me. "Are you sure?" He doesn't sound particularly happy about this, either. When I look up at him, his expression is tight.

"Can't you feel it?" Rylan rubs his chest. "Focus."

Malachi goes still for a long moment, but it's Wolf who speaks first. "Fuck."

I look from one of them to the other. "What? What are you talking about? What's going on?" My body has started to feel more like my own now, but the strangely light feeling inside me is still there. I clutch Malachi's arms. "Malachi?"

"A long time before I was born, the seraphim were hunted to extinction by the other supernatural creatures." Malachi's arms tense around me. "Or so everyone thought."

I'd heard of seraphim, of course, but I thought they were just another fictional part of the humans' religion. No one ever talks about them as if they were *real.* "Why?"

"Among their abilities is one that links them with their partners." Once again, it's Rylan who answers. "It might have started out as some kind of mating bond, but they used it to create courts of supernaturals around them. A seraph could do whatever they wanted to a bonded supernatural and that supernatural couldn't fight back, couldn't harm them in return, couldn't break free. Vampires, in particular, are susceptible."

"I heard they had godlike powers." Wolf sounds uncharacteristically serious. "There's a reason they scare the shit out of the humans, even if history has defanged them out of sheer self-preservation."

I start to pull away from Malachi, but he hugs me tighter to his chest. His voice lowers, deepens. "It doesn't matter."

"The longer she lives, the stronger the bond will grow." Rylan scrubs at his chest as if he can dig through flesh and yank the bond out by its roots. "The best bet we have is to scatter and get as far away as fast as we can before she calls us back."

What they're describing is a monster. If I'm a seraph, that means *I'm* a monster. The only thing I've ever wanted is freedom, and if what they're saying is correct, then freedom is the very thing I've stolen from them. "I'm sorry," I whisper.

"It's not your fault." Malachi climbs off the bed, taking me with him. "Can you stand?"

"Yes." I'm not sure if I'm lying, but I lock my knees to ensure I stay on my feet when he releases me.

Malachi points at the other two vampires. "Don't move."

Rylan shakes his head as Malachi leaves the room and looks at Wolf. "Run. This is going to be your only chance."

Wolf sits up and eyes me. "Nah, I'm good. This is the most excitement I've had in centuries."

"It will be your downfall."

"You're all doom and gloom. Look at her." He waves a hand at me. "*Think*, Rylan. I heard the stories of seraphim, too. The bond is annoying, but only in the hands of a tyrant. Think about what else she'll be capable of if she lives long enough."

"You're making some large assumptions."

I wrap my arms around myself and try not to shake. "Rylan's right. You should leave. I don't want..." My breath hitches. "I know what it's like not to have your freedom. I don't want to do that to you."

"See." Wolf laughs. "Not so tyrannical, is she?"

Rylan seems unmoved. "People change."

"Then run." Wolf shrugs. "Me? I'm tired of being hunted. Cornelius only has two other kids; neither of them have managed to pop a baby vampire out and become heir. With her seraph blood, I'll bet she's just as fertile as her mother was."

I blink. "Um, what?" I realize what he's suggesting and shake my head. "It'll never work." Sometime over the history of vampires, the tradition began that in order for a bloodline vampire to officially become heir, they had to procreate to prove they could continue the line should it fail elsewhere. That was back when they were slightly more plentiful, when three of the bloodlines hadn't been pruned down to one or two vampires. My father still holds to the tradition, but I've never really worried about it too much because it doesn't affect me. "I'm a bastard."

"Only because you didn't have a recognized magic until now. If you show up with a baby and start flashing seraph magic about, all we have to do is kill him to take over the colony." Wolf grins. "That's my kind of fun."

Rylan shakes his head. "She's right. It'll never work."

Malachi walks through the door, my suitcase in hand. "Sounds like the beginnings of a plan."

"More like a dream." Rylan looks at me and then away, as if he can't stand the sight of me. "We have a narrow window to get out of here unscathed. Let's not waste it. We'll deal with this later."

Guilt clamps around me. I want to be happy that I was wrong, that I really *do* have magic, but the price seems too high. I never wanted to tie these vampires to me, not in a way that defies their free will.

I never want to be my father.

I slowly dress in the clothes Malachi hands me. No answers have presented themselves by the time I pull on my boots. "Rylan's right. You should leave me. If there's some kind of geographical limit on this—"

"There's not," Rylan says flatly. "As long as you're alive, there will be a pull on us to return to your side."

I spin on him. "This was *your* idea. I didn't ask for this. I didn't set out to trap you or bond with you or whatever the hell has happened. Stop looking at me like this is my fault."

He opens his mouth and I half expect him to cut me down with a few icy words. Instead he sighs. "You're right. Sorry."

I blink. Holy shit, that was an actual apology. I glance at Malachi, but he looks just as taken aback as I am. He gives himself a shake. "Get dressed. We leave in two."

Rylan and Wolf blur out of the room. I take a deep breath and turn to Malachi. "You—"

"Stop telling me to leave you behind. It's not going to happen." He dresses in a pair of jeans, boots, and a long-sleeved shirt. Malachi pulls me into my arms, which is right around the time I realize I'm shaking again. "Not because of a mystical bond, either, so get that out of your head."

"You don't know what I'm thinking." That was exactly what I was thinking.

He gives me a squeeze. "We'll figure out a plan once we get out of here. Give me that long, okay?"

"Are you asking me or telling me?"

His lips curve. "Would you rather I toss you over my shoulder and just take you with me?"

Kind of.

Except, no, I wouldn't. I wanted a choice, and now I have one. Really, there's only one option. If my father realizes what I am, he'll try to kill me. Or, more likely, he'll try to break me so he can use me to boost his own power. Neither option is good for me. At least with these three, I have a chance. Hell, I have more than a chance.

First, we have to get out of this house.

Two minutes later, we're at the front door. Malachi tosses my suitcase to Wolf and hefts me into his arms. When I start to protest, he gives me a look. "Seraph or not, you can't keep up."

Damn it, but he's right. "Okay."

He looks at Wolf and Rylan. "Where to?"

"New York." Rylan glances at the sky. "We can get there in half a day or so, and even if he sends his trackers, it will be difficult to find us among that many humans."

Malachi nods. "Lead the way."

He moves at a quick lope across the grounds, not quite blurring. When we reach the edge of the property, Wolf leaps over the seven-foot iron fence as if it's nothing. Rylan follows suit. Malachi hesitates and then we're airborne. He tenses as we pass over the top, but nothing happens. The blood ward really is broken.

He gives that rusty laugh of his when he lands on the other side. "Freedom."

"Not quite," Rylan says.

"Close enough for me."

We take off into the night, the cool air whipping against my face. I look over Malachi's shoulder in time to see flames licking through the windows of the house we just abandoned. They spread preternaturally fast, consuming the roof in giant bites. Something gives way and a piece of the house collapses. There will be no rebuilding that particular cage.

Malachi and I really are free. Or as free as we can be while my father still lives.

I open my eyes, resolve settling over me. No matter what else happens with these three men, one thing is certain.

For us to be safe, we have to kill my father.

And I have to be pregnant before we can do it.

KEEP READING FOR A LOOK AT *HEIR* BY KATEE ROBERT

1

I CAN FEEL MALACHI'S HEARTBEAT. IT THROBS IN MY chest, a steady thump that would be reassuring if it wasn't so foreign. After all, it's not as if I'm lounging with my head on his chest the way I have many times in the last month. Malachi isn't even in the house.

He's across the county, the miles stretching between us.

I rub the back of my hand against my sternum, but if the last four weeks have taught me anything, it's that the sensation of multiple hearts nestled up against mine is magical in nature rather than physical. Malachi assures me that I'll get used to it eventually, which might actually be reassuring if his dark eyes weren't worried every time he looks at me. Better than Rylan, who won't look at me at all. I still don't understand why he hasn't left our little nest and taken his chances on his own. I don't understand him.

And Wolf?

Wolf, true to form, offered to carve open my chest to relieve me of the sensation.

"Stop it."

I don't look over as Rylan's icy words cut through the stillness of the loft. "You're talking to me now? How novel." I drop my hand and then have to curl it into a fist to resist going back to rubbing my sternum when Malachi's heartbeat kicks up a notch. The feeling in my chest intensifies, signaling proximity. "He's coming."

"About time," Rylan mutters.

At that, I finally face him. "It's been a month. Leave if you hate it with me that much."

"I would if I could." He practically hurls the words at me. His hand goes to his chest, mirroring me. He looks just as perfectly put together as he has from the moment I met him, his dark hair cut short on the silvered temples, his endless supply of suits without a wrinkle out of place. The only time I've seen him remotely rumpled was the night we all fucked, subsequently awakening my powers and landing us in this mess.

Together.

Whether we like it or not.

"Just kill me then. It's what you wanted from the beginning."

His eyes flash silver, the only sign that I've gotten beneath his skin. I shouldn't be so petty as to enjoy aggravating Rylan, but he's like a wall of knives I brush against with every movement. Malachi and Wolf might not be overly comfortable being tied to me, but at least they *like* me a little. Rylan's hated me from the start—a very mutual sentiment—and now we can't escape each other.

"Would that I could." He turns and stalks to the balcony doors, pausing to strip and systematically fold his clothing over the chair set there for what I assume is entirely that purpose.

I know what's coming, and as such, I should look away. But I've had so few pleasures in my life that I find myself unable to resist a single one, no matter the source. A naked Rylan is a pleasure, what comes next even more so.

He's gorgeous in an entirely different way from Malachi and Wolf. His suits do a good job of masking his strength, but out of them, he looks nearly as big as Malachi. He also has little dimples at the top of his ass that, despite myself, I want to lick. As much as I'd like to blame the bond for that, the truth is that I found this asshole attractive even before the night the bond snapped into place.

He steps out the doors and there's—I'm not sure how to explain it—a ripple, almost. As if reality gives a little shudder, a tiny tear, and then Rylan is gone and a giant black bird perches on the balcony in his place. A flap of its massive wings and he's gone, flinging himself out into the darkness.

He's moving quickly in the opposite direction Malachi is coming from, putting miles between us with ease. I feel each one like a nail driven into my chest. I hate it. I *want* him gone, but the more distance he puts between us, the greater the urge to demand he return.

To force him to return.

I stomp down on the urge and turn away from the balcony. I don't care what Rylan says about seraphim. I don't care that I can no longer deny that I'm one of them. I don't care about their history of bonding with and abusing vampires. Doing that intentionally would make me no worse than my monster of a father, and *that* is something I'll never do.

Death is preferable.

I can feel Wolf downstairs, likely painting again. The man holds multitudes and while I can appreciate the beauty behind his art, it's highly disturbing. Wolf is chaos personified, and that truth is even more apparent when he paints. He might kiss me or try to cut my throat on our next meeting. I never know. He scares me, but a small, secret part of me likes it. I feel particularly *alive* when I'm dancing on the blade edge with Wolf.

I don't want that right now. I'm too tired, too frustrated. Wolf, predator that he is, will pick up on it immediately, and he won't be able to resist testing me. Testing the bond. It exhausts me just thinking about going a round with him right now.

We might have spent the last month together, but I should know better than to lean on these vampires. Even Malachi, for all his declarations of intent, hasn't known me nearly long enough to actually mean anything he says. More, considering the possibility of a future together is a far cry from agreeing to a bond that only death will sever.

I am surrounded by men, but I'm just as alone as I was in my father's compound. Separate. Other. Alternatively a threat and prey, depending on who's around. The only thing I ever wanted was freedom, and it's the one thing I'll never have.

Gods, I'm a little ray of sunshine tonight.

I move through the upper floors of the house that is our most recent lodgings. Despite Malachi's intentions of losing ourselves in the city, the plan fell through almost immediately. It took my father's people less than twelve hours to find us the first time. Since then, we've had to get increasingly creative, avoiding any properties directly linked to Wolf or Rylan and moving regularly. It still isn't enough to grant us true peace, but at least we're staying ahead of my father's hounds.

Barely.

The air shifts behind me, but I don't need to look to know who it is. Malachi. When we first met, he had a habit of surprising me by appearing unexpectedly without a sound. Now that we're bonded, he'll never be able to sneak up on me again. None of them will. That knowledge should reassure me, should offer some kind of layer of safety, but it's simply a reminder of how much has changed in such a short time.

"Do you think he knew?"

Malachi doesn't ask who I'm referencing. "I doubt it. Even if she was like you and tasted different than humans do, there are a lot of monsters in our world. Knowing your father, he wouldn't have risked bedding her if he suspected she had even a hint of seraph blood."

She. My mother. The source of my seraph powers that awoke a month ago in a bed filled to the brim with sex and blood, the chain that now binds me to these three bloodline vampires.

Not every vampire in our world is graced with magic. Those turned might get the near-immortal life spans, but that's the best of it. Even those naturally born barely have a leg up over the turned vampires.

No, the true power lies with the seven bloodline families, each with a specialization they pass from parents to children. There are other perks, including pleasurable bites, but the real focus is the magic. My father can get anyone to do anything he wants as long as they're in the same room and he's able to speak. He can also use his glamour to shift his appearance.

And now I have three bloodline vampires linked to me. Malachi with his fire. Wolf with his blood magic. Rylan with his shape-shifting. Practically an army of three, all vested in keeping me alive, because if I die, there's a decent chance I'll drag them all to hell with me. Aside from my father, little can touch me now. If I were a different person, maybe I'd be elated.

I never wanted any of it.

Malachi closes the distance between us and wraps his arms around me, tugging me back against his large body. If not for the way he sometimes looks at me, I might allow myself to sink into these little intimate moments. To believe that the future holds even a sliver of happiness for me.

"You're thinking too hard." Malachi rests his chin on the top of my head. "You and Rylan have been sniping at each other again, haven't you?"

"I didn't want this," I whisper. I can feel Rylan winging his way farther and farther from the house—from me. Eventually, he'll reach the limits of our bond just like he has countless times in the last month, and it will snap at him until he turns back. "Why can't he understand I hate this even more than you all do?"

"He's got a long and complicated history with the seraphim. When your memory is as long as Rylan's, it's difficult to get past old beliefs. Old fears." Malachi delves his hands beneath my shirt to bracket my waist. I try to resent that the feel of his hands on my skin instantly unwinds some of my tension. I try...and I fail. I want to blame *this* on the bond, too, but my attraction to Malachi has been there from the moment we met and only seems to grow stronger with time.

With a sigh, I lean back more firmly against him, letting him coast his hands up my sides. "I didn't want this."

"I know." He shifts to press a kiss to my temple, my cheekbone, my jaw. "Mina."

"Yes." An answer and permission, all rolled into one. Rylan may be staying as far from me as he can manage. Wolf is as changeable as the wind, wild for me and avoiding me by turns. Only Malachi is consistent in this.

I wish I could believe that it's simply because he wants me.

If I were anyone else, maybe I could. But I'm not. I'm the daughter of Cornelius Lancaster, the last bloodline vampire of his line. Up until a month ago, I was a freak, a powerless dhampir. Half human, half vampire, somehow missing the power that should come along with that mixing of vampire with human. Useless except as a pawn in my father's schemes, as a womb to fill with another bloodline.

I have power now, but that doesn't make me safe.

If my father discovers that I have not one but *three* bloodline vampires linked to me, he'll use me as a tool to bring them to their knees. I might not want to take their freedom and willpower, but he'll be only too happy to in order to boost his own power. Killing him might be possible, but it won't solve the problem, not when I have other half siblings who are ready and willing to step into his shoes.

We have one chance to avoid being hunted until the end of time.

I have to become my father's heir.

The only way to do *that* is to get pregnant before any of my half siblings do. Not exactly an easy feat when some of them have been trying since before I was born. Not to mention I don't even know how vampire and seraph and human mix together. Rylan claims it's possible—even probable—that I can conceive and quickly. I'm not so sure.

"Mina." Malachi's lips brush my throat. "It will work out."

"You don't know that."

"No more than you know that it *won't* work out." He kisses my neck. "Let me make you feel good for a little bit."

Let him make me feel good. Let him have another go at getting me pregnant.

I exhale slowly. At this rate, my racing thoughts aren't going to slow down without extreme measures. "Bite me."

Malachi, gods bless him, doesn't hesitate. He sinks his fangs into my skin. Just like that, every thought turns to mist in my head. I melt back against him. Every pull as he drinks from me has pleasure curling through my body. Yes, this. This is what I crave right now.

I reach back and fumble at his pants. I need him inside me and I need it now. "Please."

He withdraws long enough to pull my shirt over my head and skim off my pants. His clothing quickly follows, and he wastes no time carrying me to a nearby couch. It's as sturdy as all the other furniture in this house, as if it were built for giants instead of regular people. Malachi sets me down and goes to his knees in front of me.

In this position, he feels even larger than he is. Broad shoulders that taper down to a slim waist. Muscles strong enough to punch his way through concrete walls without breaking a sweat. Scars upon scars, his outsides matching my insides. I reach out and press my hand to the mangled flesh over his heart where someone tried to carve it out. He still hasn't told me that story. Maybe he never will.

I abandon that line of thinking and dig my hands into his hair. It's just as long and dark as mine, though he's got a bit more wave in it. "I need you."

"Not yet." He presses me back against the couch and kisses his way down my stomach, his beard scraping against skin already overly sensitized by his bite. "I'm ravenous for you, Mina."

This. This right here is why I can't quite believe Malachi is only in this because he has no choice. We might be trapped together, have been trapped since the moment we met: first in that old house by my father's blood ward and now by the bond that strums between us with every beat of our hearts. If it was only the bond, Malachi would fuck me and nothing else. I'd hardly complain if that was all we did.

Instead, he's bringing me pleasure in a multitude of other ways every chance he gets.

In particular, he loves eating my pussy as much as I enjoy his mouth on me.

His breath ghosts against my clit and I shiver. "Well, if you insist."

Movement behind him has me startling. I was so focused on Malachi, I didn't feel Wolf approaching. He stands outlined by the doorframe, his lean form clothed in his normal eccentric mix of dark pants, a graphic T-shirt with a band I've never heard of, and suspenders. He gives me a feral grin. "You started playing without me."

Malachi doesn't lift his head, each word vibrating against my heated flesh. "Get over here, then."

ABOUT THE AUTHOR

Katee Robert is a *New York Times* and *USA Today* bestselling author of contemporary romance and romantic suspense. *Entertainment Weekly* calls her writing "unspeakably hot." Her books have sold over a million copies. She lives in the Pacific Northwest with her husband, children, a cat who thinks he's a dog, and two Great Danes who think they're lap dogs. You can visit her at kateerobert.com or on Twitter @katee_robert.